SADIE'S DREAM

Patti Jo Moore

Published by Forget Me Not Romances, a division of Winged Publications

ISBN-13: 978-1-947523-63-0
ISBN-10: 1-947523-63-5

DEDICATION

Sadie's Dream is dedicated to my son-in-law, Shaun Manny. You add so much joy and laughter to our family, and I love you like a son.

I'm thankful to my Lord and Savior Jesus Christ, for loving me and graciously giving me my dreams. May my words always honor Him.

Chapter One

Coastal Georgia 1900

Sadie Elizabeth Perkins could not believe her ears. She stared across the store's counter at the clerk in amazement. Surely Dolly Hatcher didn't have her facts straight.

"I know it's surprising, Sadie dear. But that's what I heard this morning. A resort hotel is to be built here in Riverview. Construction should begin this summer, although I don't know the particular date." The middle-aged woman lifted her chin, as though she'd revealed the location for hidden treasure.

Shaking her head, Sadie reached to retrieve her purchases. The bag of sugar, cans of beans and corn, and the loaf of bread fit snugly into Sadie's wicker basket, although heavier than it appeared.

"Yes, Mrs. Hatcher, this is surprising news. Why would anyone want to build a resort hotel in our little town? We're not on the Atlantic Ocean, and we don't have anything spectacular to offer tourists." Sadie clutched her basket with both hands, eager to be on her way home.

"Well, from what I heard, the fact that our town sits on the banks of the Altamaha River is supposed to be the selling feature. Tourists could arrive either by water or land, so I reckon the builders are thinking that might bring in lots of northern folks wanting to visit our warmer climates. Especially during the winter months. But I'll admit I was surprised too when I first heard the news." Dolly Hatcher smoothed a hand along her apron.

Sadie took a step toward the door, but realized the store clerk had more information to share.

With a wink, Dolly leaned closer to Sadie and lowered her voice. "Mr. Watkins shared the news with me, so I feel certain it's not gossip. He's such a smart man and has business dealings over in Savannah—that's where the developers are." She clamped her lips together as though she'd spoken too much.

"Anyway, Sadie dear, I'll be sure to keep you posted when I hear more news. Please tell your papa that Fred and I inquired about him." She gave Sadie a kind smile before turning to another customer who'd stepped up to the counter.

After waving to Fred Hatcher, who was placing cans on a nearby shelf, Sadie hurried outside into the sunny March afternoon. She stepped to her bicycle parked underneath a large oak tree, as a squirrel scurried up to the leafy branches. Positioning the wicker basket on the handlebar, Sadie lifted her skirt to climb onto the vehicle.

How she loved riding her bicycle, especially when the weather was pleasant as it was today. She was thankful it wasn't one of her days to work at the local library, although she enjoyed her job. But on her off days, the twenty-five-year old tried to complete her household chores so she could spend as much time as possible riding around her small town.

She pedaled down the road away from Hatcher's Store. Warming her face, the sun streamed down between puffy clouds that reminded her of Sea Island cotton. Sadie's long chestnut mane lifted from her shoulders as she rode along in the refreshing air. She drew in a deep breath and pondered the news Dolly Hatcher had shared with her.

Without warning, a small brown object darted across the road in front of her, and with a gasp she swerved to avoid the animal. Sadie's bicycle veered to the right to avoid the rabbit that hopped safely to the left side of the road, disappearing into weeds and brush.

Gripping the handlebars, Sadie held on as her bicycle careened off the road, turned completely over to the right, tossing her from the seat and into the weeds. Dazed, she sat on the rough, hard ground surrounded by tall grasses and prickly bushes.

Drawing in a ragged breath, Sadie hoped no one had witnessed her fall. Although a bit stunned, she didn't think any bones were broken. However, the fall would leave her sore and bruised. She must look like a fool sitting there by the roadside, her overturned bicycle resting on her legs and her grocery items scattered on the ground.

Attempting to hoist herself from the ground, Sadie froze when a voice called out to her. A *male* voice.

"Miss, are you all right?" The question came from the direction she'd traveled. She turned her head toward the left.

A dark-haired man ran toward Sadie, his face showing obvious concern. When he was a few feet away, he slowed his pace as though not wanting to frighten her.

Sadie's heart pounded and she felt ridiculous sitting amongst the weeds. Her mind swirled with questions. Who was this man? Had he seen her fall?

Without another word, the man stepped toward her and lifted the bicycle off Sadie's legs, then stood the vehicle upright and set the kickstand. Turning to face her, the stranger gently took her hands in his and brought her to a standing position. His eyes traveled the length of her before his gaze locked with Sadie's.

"You appear to be okay, Miss. But how do you feel?"

Standing only a few feet away, the stranger was without a doubt the most handsome man Sadie had ever seen. Tall and broad-shouldered, there was a ruggedness about him—in a gentlemanly sort of way. His eyes were deep-set and dark, closely matching his head of black hair that had been tousled from his run down the road.

"Ma'am? Are you okay?" The man inclined his head toward her, concern growing in his eyes.

Sadie realized she hadn't yet responded to his first question. Her heart thumped loudly. She had to answer, or he'd think she wasn't quite right in the head.

She nodded and looked up at him. In a shaky voice, she replied, "Y-Yes, thank you for helping me. I-I'm fine now. A rabbit darted across the road, and I didn't want to hit the poor little thing." She peered down at her skirt and brushed away pieces of dirt and bits of dried grass. What a mess she must appear.

He grinned. "I'm Shaun O'Leary, ma'am, of Savannah. I'm here in Riverview on business, and was heading into the general store down the road when I noticed you taking a tumble. But I'm glad you're okay."

A warmth crept up her face. Sadie wished she wasn't cursed with blushing so easily. *Why must this man standing before her be so very handsome?* Moistening her lips, she smiled and attempted to keep her voice steady while replying.

"I'm Miss Sadie Perkins. Thank you again for helping me, Mr. O'Leary. You're very kind."

Shaun O'Leary arched an eyebrow at her last comment, as though somewhat amused.

A distant rumble of thunder sounded, and Sadie abruptly lifted her head toward the sky. She knew she'd best be heading home. There was no way she wanted to be outdoors if a sudden storm struck. She almost shivered at the very thought.

"It was nice meeting you, Miss Perkins. Please be

careful riding home." Shaun O'Leary smiled and nodded at her again, then stepped away to return in the direction of the general store.

Drawing in a deep breath, Sadie climbed onto her bicycle, relieved that her rescuer didn't remain there. She must keep her hands steady and her gaze on the road.

As she pedaled away from the attractive man from Savannah, Sadie had the distinct feeling he was watching her travel down the road.

~ ~ ~ ~

Sadie arrived home just in time. No sooner had she wheeled her bicycle into the storage shed than the first drops of rain began falling. Hurrying up the steps to the front porch of the cottage she shared with her father, Sadie clutched her basket of grocery items with one hand and lifted her skirt with the other. She had already taken one tumble today—she certainly didn't want to trip and fall again.

Stepping into the cottage, Sadie jumped when a loud clap of thunder roared outside. She slammed and locked the door behind her. With her eyes darting around the living room, Sadie searched for her beloved cats. She must make certain Moses and Levi were safely indoors during this storm.

Bustling into the kitchen to put away the groceries, Sadie released a sigh of relief when she spotted both felines curled up under the kitchen table.

"Hello, kitties. I guess you both feel safer under the table with this storm raging outdoors. I don't blame you a bit." She chuckled at the cats' sleepy yawns.

After putting away her items, Sadie kept busy preparing a pot of stew for supper. Even though her father wasn't due home from his job for a few more hours, she wanted the stew to be ready to eat when he arrived.

Besides, she always made a point of keeping herself

occupied during a storm. Memories of the horrible hurricane of 1898 still lingered in her mind, although she tried not to dwell on it. The lives lost and the damage done along the Atlantic coast had affected so many, including families she knew. A shudder ran through Sadie and she shoved those awful memories away.

While chopping carrots and potatoes for the stew, Sadie's mind replayed Dolly Hatcher's news in the store that day. A resort hotel to be built in Riverview—what an unusual idea. Sadie planned to share the news with Papa and hear his thoughts. Most likely he'd agree with her. Who would ever think of having a fancy hotel in their small town? It didn't make sense.

Thirty minutes later the pot of stew simmered on the stove, and Sadie was ready to sit and read, her favorite indoor pastime. As thunder rumbled and lightning zigzagged across the sky, Sadie felt safe indoors, curled up in the large, overstuffed chair in the living room, clasping a novel.

Yet for some reason, she couldn't stay focused on the story. Her mind kept returning to the handsome stranger who'd assisted her earlier that day. In addition, her right leg was sore and throbbing, so she couldn't get comfortable. She'd have to be careful and not limp around her papa. He would worry if he knew about the tumble from her bicycle.

After Horace Perkins arrived home from work, he joined Sadie at the kitchen table.

The aroma of simmering stew filled the room, and the tired man sniffed the air. "Ah, you spoil your papa." Lowering himself into the chair, he reached up to rub his left shoulder.

"It's only stew, Papa. But I do hope you'll enjoy it. And I see you're rubbing that shoulder again. So it's still bothering you, I suppose?" Her brow furrowed, she set a ceramic bowl of hot stew in front of her father. She paused a moment before getting her own bowl.

Horace chuckled and shook his head. "Now Sadie, no

need for you to be frettin' over me. It's just that same ol' pain I get now and then. Most likely arthritis flarin' up and gets aggravated from my work at the lumber mill. I'll be fine, so get your bowl of stew so we can bless this fine meal and commence to eatin'." Aware of her father's grin, she spooned up stew for herself.

After Horace offered a blessing for their simple meal of stew, cornbread, and tea, the pair chatted about the storm they'd had that afternoon.

"I'm thankful it had blown over by the time you left work to come home. I don't like you being outdoors when it's so bad." Sadie took a sip of her tea and tried to hide her feelings of concern. She worried about her father—he was getting older and the physical job he had was taking a toll on his body.

He grinned. "The good Lord watches over your ol' papa, Sadie girl. Just like He watches over you." He paused, but when he spoke again his voice was thick with emotion. "I don't know for sure exactly how heaven is, but I like to think of your Mama sittin' up there, lookin' down on both of us too." His eyes misted, and he ducked his head and sniffed.

Even though Elizabeth Perkins had been gone for ten years, they missed her something terrible. Succumbing to pneumonia when Sadie was only fifteen, Elizabeth was a woman loved by all who knew her. The only comfort her loved ones had was knowing Elizabeth now resided in heaven, and her husband and daughter would see her again one day. Still, there were times when Horace or Sadie became emotional, so they tried to boost each other and forge ahead.

Sadie fought tears that threatened. She must be strong for Papa. Clearing her throat, she attempted to have an upbeat tone in her voice.

"Papa, I heard such interesting news today, and wondered if you'd heard anything at the lumber mill. Mrs. Hatcher told me that a resort hotel is to be built here in

Riverview. I'm still surprised, because our little town is certainly not a tourist attraction." Sadie was relieved that her father seemed back to his usual self rather than overcome with sadness.

"A hotel, you say? My, that is interestin'. No, I haven't heard anything about such news, but I'll sure keep my ears open. Them fellars at the mill remind me of a bunch of hens sometimes—they get to talkin' about things and I get downright tickled. I feel sure once they get wind of this news, they'll be cackling up a storm." Horace chuckled, and Sadie joined him.

When the meal was over, Horace thanked Sadie and headed toward the living room to read the daily newspaper. He reached up and rubbed his shoulder as he ambled out of the kitchen.

"Papa, how about I ask Doc Wilson to take a look at your shoulder? Perhaps he can give you some liniment to rub on it and help ease the pain. There's no need for you to keep hurting so much. Especially with the kind of work you do at the lumber mill. Tomorrow when I leave my job at the library, I can stop by his office."

With difficulty, Horace turned around, a serious look on his weathered face. Then he grinned and winked at her. "I want to say no to your suggestion. But I have a feelin' that you're going to keep hounding your papa until I let you talk to the doc. So I reckon when you get a chance you can tell him about my shoulder. But he's a busy man, and this isn't an emergency. We don't want to trouble Doc Wilson."

Sadie giggled and scurried over to her father, then planted a quick kiss on his cheek. "You're as important as any of Doc Wilson's other patients. I'll try to speak with him tomorrow afternoon. He'll have something that will help."

Sadie returned to her dishes in the kitchen and thought about her fall from the bicycle earlier that day. Her leg was hurting even worse than it had that afternoon, and she'd had to be careful not to limp when her father was nearby.

today?" The fairly plump woman wiped her hands on the apron she wore. Her fair-skinned face held a hint of pink, no doubt from bustling around in the kitchen and being near the hot stove.

Shaun returned the housekeeper's smile, amazed at how warmly the woman always greeted him. In fact, she usually seemed happier to see him than members of the O'Leary family did. "The trip went well, Maude. Thank you for asking. The town of Riverview seems like a nice area—right on the banks of the Altamaha River. I'm sorry I don't have a gift for you—perhaps if I go on a longer trip in the future, I can bring back a surprise for you." He grinned at the older woman, thinking back to times he'd brought her small trinkets or boxes of candy. She was always more than appreciative of his kind gestures.

"Listen to you, young man. Now I've told you that although I certainly do appreciate the gifts you've given me, I never expect gifts from you or any member of the O'Leary family."

Sadly, Shaun couldn't think of a time anyone else in his family had surprised Maude with a gift—even a small token. He also knew his parents and even his younger sister Margaret viewed Maude as merely the "hired help"— something that had always troubled Shaun.

True, Maude was employed by the O'Leary family, but not only did she go above her daily work requirements, she was dependable, caring, and kind. Shaun had often thought the housekeeper deserved a crown for enduring his mother's harsh tone and criticism.

With a grin, he spoke gently. "I know you don't expect any gifts. But I realize you don't have an easy task being in the employ of the O'Leary family." Without a doubt the housekeeper would know the primary person to whom he was referring, although Maude was too polite to reply aloud.

She smoothed her apron and held her head proudly. "I'm honored to work for the O'Leary family, and now I best be gettin' back to the kitchen, because if I burn the roast and potatoes, the O'Leary family isn't going to be happy with me." With a chuckle, Maude hurried back to the kitchen. When she reached the doorway, she called over her shoulder. "It should be about thirty minutes until the meal is ready, Mr. Shaun."

He thanked her and decided to head upstairs and rest a bit before the meal. Approaching footsteps came down the stairs. He slowed his pace to allow his mother adequate time to finish descending the flight of stairs.

Colleen O'Leary held tightly to the oak banister as she took another downward step. Her pained face lit up at the sight of her son. "Hello, Shaun, I'm glad you're home in time for our evening meal. How was your day?" She finished the last few steps and stood in the hallway, several feet from him. Then a frown creased her brow and she brought a hand up to her forehead.

Shaun stepped over to his mother and placed a quick peck on her cheek. "Hello, Mother. My day went well, thank you for asking. Do you have one of your headaches again?" Unfortunately, she had them frequently. One of the first indications was simply bringing her hand up to her forehead. Did his mother make that gesture in order to gain sympathy from her family? He couldn't imagine how a hand to the forehead would do anything to lessen the pain.

Colleen O'Leary released a long sigh and gazed into her son's eyes. "Yes, I'm afraid I do. I felt fine this morning, but as the day wore on, my head began to ache and now it's almost throbbing. I had lain down earlier but decided to make sure Maude had cleaned the upstairs floors this week."

A small niggle of irritation ran through Shaun at his mother's comment. Maude had always done an excellent job and had never required anyone going behind her to check on her work. Shaun had a feeling his mother wanted to ensure that the housekeeper remembered who was in charge, and therefore followed up—although needlessly—on Maude's work.

Shaun had a strong urge to voice his feelings to his mother but decided to hold his tongue. Defending Maude would only make his mother agitated, and unfortunately Colleen O'Leary could bring a cloud over the entire household when agitated.

"Perhaps after you eat supper, your headache pain will lessen, Mother. The meal Maude is preparing smells wonderful." Shaun offered a wide smile, hoping to lighten his mother's mood at least a little. Then he patted her shoulder with his free hand and stepped around her to begin climbing the stairs to the second floor.

Colleen glanced over her shoulder and turned toward the kitchen. "I hope eating will help me feel better, son. And I also hope that Maude doesn't overcook the roast. The last time she prepared one, it was rather tough." With a "tsk" sound, Colleen continued on toward the kitchen.

Shaun reached the second floor, turned to the right and walked to his bedroom. He'd been grateful that his parents had welcomed him to live in their house again after he became widowed, but it hadn't been without its challenges.

He was finding more and more often he had to resist the urge to snap a retort at his mother when she made condescending remarks. He'd finally learned that doing so accomplished nothing good, only adding fuel to the fire.

Stretching out on his bed for a few minutes of rest, Shaun's mind replayed his visit to Riverview. But instead of contemplating the purpose of his trip, all he could think about was the woman he'd assisted. Sadie Perkins. For some reason, Shaun couldn't get the image of her face out of his mind.

~ ~ ~ ~

Maude's roast beef and potatoes were delicious and not a bit overcooked, Shaun noted with delight as he eyed his mother cutting into her slice of meat. The O'Leary's evening meal had begun on a positive note as the housekeeper had placed the platters of steaming food before the family. Maude had even baked a pan of her feather-light biscuits, one of Shaun's favorites. He hadn't realized how hungry he was until biting into the biscuit that seemed to melt in his mouth.

Apparently his mother's headache had dissipated because she made no mention of it during the meal, so Shaun didn't ask. Better to keep the conversation as pleasant as possible.

After a few casual comments about the weather, silence ensued for a few minutes, the clatter of silverware against the china being the only sound.

Shaun enjoyed a few bites of his meal, then eyed his younger sister, Margaret, seated across the table from him. "So Maggie, how's your job at the bank?" He used the nickname he'd given her when she was a child, and her friends had begun calling her by that name also. In fact, Shaun's parents were the only ones who still used their daughter's given name, most likely because Margaret sounded more formal than Maggie.

She swallowed her bite of potatoes and grinned at her brother. "It's going fairly well. But with our father stopping by the bank to check on me, I have to make certain I'm keeping my nose to the grindstone." Maggie giggled and winked at her brother before casting a quick glance at her father.

George O'Leary, for all his serious demeanor and formalities, seemed to melt like butter where his daughter was concerned. Maggie had always been able to talk her father into agreeing to anything she wanted, much to the chagrin of Colleen O'Leary.

Shaun had always assumed it was because Maggie had been very ill as an infant, and George O'Leary had been fearful of losing his only daughter. Thankfully she'd recovered and since then had been healthy.

George lifted his coffee cup to his mouth and suppressed a smile at Maggie. After swallowing, he said, "I only want to assure myself that my daughter is doing her required duties at the bank. After all, the bank manager granted us a tremendous favor in hiring you, Margaret dear." He returned to eating, and silence resumed at the table.

As everyone was finishing the meal, Colleen wiped her mouth and cleared her throat, signifying she had something important to say. Shaun braced himself because he had the sneaking suspicion that whatever his mother said would somehow involve him.

"Shaun, dear, you seem to be doing quite well in your employment with your father's business. You also seem to be building your finances, which is to be commended." All eyes were on Colleen. She paused, cleared her throat again, and continued. "As your mother—who only wants the best for you—I think it would be a delightful idea for you to begin courting one of the young ladies here in Savannah. There are still several who have remained single and I feel certain any of those ladies would be honored to be courted by such a fine man as you. After all, you've been widowed a respectable amount of time since Grace departed." Colleen's voice softened and she lowered her eyes. "May she rest in peace."

With each sentence his mother had spoken, Shaun bristled. It had been all he could do to remain silent during her spiel.

Colleen gazed directly at Shaun, awaiting his response. No, demanded his response would be more appropriate.

"Thank you for your input, Mother. The ladies you're referencing hold no interest for me. Although they are lovely young debutantes from well-to-do families, I could never pursue one of them if I had no real feelings for the woman herself. I'm sure you wouldn't want me to marry someone simply so the O'Leary name could be joined with one of

Savannah's fine, upstanding families, now would you?" Shaun made no effort to conceal the smirk on his lips. The silence in the room felt thick enough to slice with one of Maude's carving knives.

Pushing away from the table, Shaun glanced toward the kitchen and hoped Maude heard him. "Thank you for the delicious meal, Maude. You outdid yourself this evening."

The housekeeper bustled into the dining room, holding a steaming pie that had just come from the oven. Setting the dessert on the mahogany buffet along one wall, Maude then turned to Shaun in wide-eyed curiosity. "Why Mr. Shaun, don't you want a slice of cherry pie?"

Shaun managed a smile for the kind woman. "No thank you, Maude, although I'm sure it's tasty. Please save a piece and I'll enjoy it tomorrow. Good evening." Before leaving the room, Shaun noticed the stunned looks on the faces of his family.

His pulse raced and his head throbbed. The delectable meal he'd enjoyed minutes earlier was now doing flips in his stomach. He stepped onto the front porch, resisting the urge to slam the door behind him.

Heading toward the street, Shaun turned left and followed the sidewalk to the next block. Maybe the chilly evening air would calm him. Why did he allow his mother's comments to upset him so?

Reaching the end of the second block, he turned to his left and continued walking. With his mother's condescending remarks too fresh in his mind, Shaun strode toward a destination. Riley's, the tavern closest to Shaun's neighborhood, seemed to beckon him. And in his current mood, Shaun was not about to ignore the invitation.

Chapter Two

"And the lovely maiden and the handsome prince lived happily ever after." Sadie closed the book and smiled down at the group of children huddled at her feet. Reading to the children was her favorite part of her job at the library.

"That was a good story, Miss Sadie. Thank you." Young Bethany Martin looked up at Sadie with wide blue eyes. The little girl was still smiling even though the story had ended.

"You are welcome, Bethany. We'll have another story next week, so I do hope you boys and girls will join me again." Sadie watched the little ones hurry to meet their waiting mothers, who'd been talking amongst themselves next to the bookshelves.

Several women grinned and waved their thanks to Sadie before leaving the library with their children in tow. Sadie remained in the oak rocking chair for another minute, watching them leave. How she'd love to have her own children. But apparently it wasn't meant to be. Her beau had been unfaithful, and no prospects had taken his place. Besides, after much prayer, Sadie felt her calling was to be a missionary, so that's what she was focusing on.

Rising from the chair, Sadie headed toward the children's book section of the small library. She'd return the fairy tale to its proper place before going to the front counter to assist Polly White, the head librarian. Sadie was almost at the counter when the library door opened and Lucy Johnson entered. The lovely young widow, also Sadie's best friend, beamed and waved an envelope in her right hand.

"Sadie, I hate to interrupt you while you're working, but I had to share something with you." She lowered her breathless voice to a whisper. "Remember my dear Aunt Matilda?" Upon seeing her friend's puzzled expression, Lucy continued. "You know—my widowed aunt who lives at St. Simon's Island?" Now standing a mere foot from Sadie, Lucy's excitement was obvious.

Remembering the name, Sadie said, "Oh yes, I do remember when you told me about your aunt moving to St. Simon's Island after her husband passed away." Sadie's voice lowered before continuing. "How is she doing?"

Lucy practically hopped up and down. "She's doing well, and she wants us to come for a visit this spring."

Sadie was taken aback at hearing this unexpected information. "I'm glad she's doing well, but are you sure your aunt included me in her invitation? She might want to enjoy a visit with only you—since you're family."

With a playful swat of her hand toward Sadie, Lucy shook her head. "Heavens no. Aunt Matilda specifically stated in her letter that she wants me to bring my best friend—and that's you." Pausing only a moment, Lucy grinned and continued. "So what do you say? Please say you'll come with me. We'll have such a fun time, and only be gone for a few days. Your papa and your cats will be fine, and I'm certain Mrs. White will give you a few days off from your job here." Lucy gestured with her head toward the counter, where the librarian was assisting a patron.

"Well...it does sound delightful. But I'll need to know

the details and make sure Papa is agreeable to this little trip, even though I think he will be. After all, I am twenty-five now." Sadie brought a hand up to her mouth and giggled. Then with widened eyes, she whispered to Lucy, "But I'd better get back to work, or I won't have my job here any longer." She flashed a smile, feeling that Lucy's offer might prove to be just what she needed. After all, she'd been feeling in a bit of a rut lately anyway.

That evening at supper, Sadie mentioned the trip to her father. To her relief, Horace acquiesced.

"A change of scenery will be good for you, Sadie girl. You work so hard keeping house for me and also working at your library job." Then, as if reading his daughter's mind, Horace chuckled and nodded. "And don't worry about Moses and Levi. Your cats will be fed while you're away, I assure you."

Sadie hopped up from her chair and rushed around the kitchen table to hug her father. "Thank you, Papa. And Lucy said it's only for a few days, so I'll make certain to prepare some food before I leave, and you'll have plenty to eat."

Horace patted his belly and released a deep chuckle. "No worries there. I don't think your papa is going to wither away from hunger." They both laughed.

The next day Sadie pedaled her bicycle to Hatcher's Store, her mind drifting to the upcoming trip with Lucy. Even though St. Simon's Island wasn't far away from Riverview, Sadie had never been there. She tried to imagine what the area would look like from what Lucy had told her in the past, but only a vague image came to mind. Well, she'd know before long. In the meantime, there was much to do making certain to leave their kitchen well-stocked for Papa, and also preparing her trunk.

The early April breeze caressed her face. On a whim she took a different route to the store. Steering her bicycle down a tree-lined street, Sadie glanced at the large homes to her left. Although they were not mansions, they were larger than the cottage she and Papa shared.

When Sadie was a child, these houses had almost appeared as castles to her, and she often imagined royal families residing in them. Sadie giggled—such innocent foolish memories. Yet that was one of the best things about childhood, in her opinion. The ability to imagine and dream, and cling to the hope that one day those dreams would come true.

A stronger breeze whipped Sadie's hair, as though reminding her that she was no longer a child with dreams, but rather an adult whose dream was not being realized. And there was another reminder—just up ahead.

To her right sat the loveliest house of all—at least to Sadie. When she was a little girl, Sadie and her mother took walks along this street, and every time they passed this particular house, Sadie wanted to stop.

She could still hear her mother's words as though Elizabeth Perkins was alive and standing beside her. *It is a lovely house, Sadie. Perhaps when you're grown, you can live in that house someday.* Then her mother would always look down at her and smile.

Tears formed in Sadie's eyes and she blinked to keep them at bay. Then she veered to the right and stopped her bicycle. Thankfully, no one was walking past her on the sidewalk, or she might have received odd glances for rubbing her eyes with the back of her hand.

She set the kickstand on her bicycle, then walked five yards toward the house. Although she stood on the property of the vacant house, it wasn't trespassing because someday it might be hers.

There was something about the graceful structure that spoke to her, just as it had years before when Sadie and her mother took walks past the house. Why had no one purchased and restored it? She eyed the chipped paint, boards on the front porch that needed to be replaced, and shingles on the roof that were definitely past their prime.

Yet even with all the work that the structure needed, it was still beautiful to Sadie. The porch extending from one side of the house to the other, the tall windows with leaded panes, the chimneys standing proudly on the rooftop, and her favorite part—the turret along the left side of the house. She could imagine children pretending to live in a castle and using the rooms in the turret. Her children playing in her house—laughter ringing out and Sadie lovingly watching her little ones pretend to be a queen or king.

Approaching footsteps coming from her left snapped her out of the daydream all too quickly, and Sadie turned and hurried to her waiting bicycle. She glanced toward the elderly man taking a walk, and offered a polite smile.

The man nodded a greeting at her and continued his walk.

Sadie was thankful no one she knew had happened by, because more than likely she'd have to answer questions about why she was gazing at a vacant house on Willow Lane. The truth was, Sadie still had a dream involving the house. Although she'd given up on marrying and having children of her own, her prayers continued about one day opening an orphanage in the house. She would still have children to care for, and the house would be filled with laughter and love.

How she hoped that would come to pass—after she returned from the mission field. First things first, Sadie knew. But she wasn't giving up on her dream—even if the dream had been altered, thanks to being deceived by Gus Pearson.

~ ~ ~ ~

George O'Leary shook his head, his eyes blazing with anger. "That's preposterous, Shaun. Did you question the banker about who actually owns the property? Did you make the man aware that we're prepared to make a serious offer for that piece of land—along with the house located on it?" The middle-aged man paced back and forth in his office, pausing every few moments to glare at his son, standing a few feet away.

Outside on the streets of Savannah, the sounds from the passers-by drifted through the windows of Mr. O'Leary's office. Now and then the creak of carriage wheels could be heard, and for a moment, Shaun wished he was on one, rather than facing his father.

Shaun hated feeling like a young boy again, even at twenty-seven years of age. It wasn't as though he hadn't tried to get information on the property his father wanted to purchase. At the same time, Shaun had not wanted to seem overly pushy and anger the bank president. He had learned in previous dealings that when one wanted to make a purchase, it was best to keep the seller as happy as possible.

Looking at his father, Shaun attempted to keep his voice even and confident. "Yes, Father. I went over all the details exactly as you'd instructed me, but the man was quite evasive. He said the land had belonged to a certain family in Riverview for a long time, and it was unclear as to the present owners. He went on to emphasize that he highly doubted the owners would be willing to sell. At least the bank president is going to check on it, and we have another meeting scheduled for next week." Shaun only hoped that bit of information would appease his father and soften the man's stormy mood.

To Shaun's great relief, George O'Leary nodded thoughtfully and his previous glare slowly disappeared, although he looked far from pleased. After a few moments of silence, he spoke to Shaun in a more pleasant tone. "All right. I do realize you tried, but this would be an important project for our company. I'm prepared to allow you to completely oversee the plans and construction of this hotel—provided you are able to convince the banker to sell. What's the man's name again?" George's scowl had returned.

"Mr. Withers. And even though he was polite and friendly, he was far from being a pushover. The man gave me the impression that when he says something, that's it."

"Well, this Mr. Withers hasn't dealt with the O'Leary family in the past, so we shall see. It still sounds like poppycock to me that the banker isn't even certain as to the ownership of the house and property. Apparently that town doesn't handle business matters as we do here in Savannah." George O'Leary mopped his brow with a handkerchief, then looked his son in the eye again. "And one other thing. To avoid the necessity of making trips back and forth between Savannah and Riverview, it might be an excellent idea for you to find somewhere to stay in that little town. Surely they do have some type of lodging facility there?" George's tone held a bit of sarcasm.

Shaun resisted the urge to remind his father that he'd stayed the previous night in a small inn on the edge of Riverview. Instead, he nodded and replied in a calm tone. "Yes, Father. I actually noticed a boardinghouse near the Riverview Bank, so I'll inquire about a room there. I do agree about staying in Riverview rather than continuing to make constant trips between the two cities."

He wasn't going to share with his father about assisting the lovely young woman who'd tumbled from her bicycle. If Shaun stayed in Riverview even for a few days, that would increase the likelihood of seeing Miss Perkins again. At least he hoped it would.

Shaun returned to his small office to resume his daily tasks, but knew where his mind would most likely venture. Not talking with a banker in Riverview, but seeing a lovely young woman named Sadie.

~ ~ ~ ~

"I'm so excited I could burst." Lucy giggled and squeezed Sadie's hand. The two women were awaiting the ferry that would carry them over to St. Simon's Island. The morning air hung thick with humidity, but a cool breeze drifted up from the water and offered a respite.

Sadie couldn't deny that she, too, was excited about the brief trip with Lucy, but also a bit nervous. Had she left everything in order at home? Papa had assured her she'd prepared enough food for an army, and he'd also promised to feed her cats while she was away. Sadie's trunk had been packed and re-packed, so she had everything she'd need. Besides, they were only planning to be gone for five days—not even a full week.

Drawing in a deep breath, Sadie sent up a silent prayer that her father, cats, and everything at home would be fine while she was gone, then determined to focus on the sights around her. Sadie had traveled so seldom in her life and needed to make the most of this trip.

Another thought crept into Sadie's mind, but she didn't want to think about it at the moment. Her goal to become a missionary. If she truly felt called to go into mission work and travel to another country, that would involve a major journey rather than a five-day visit to an island off the Georgia coast. A long voyage across the vast Atlantic Ocean. No, Sadie couldn't dwell on those thoughts at the moment.

Lucy continued chattering, just as she'd done the entire ride from Riverview to Brunswick. Sadie had observed Lucy's father shaking his head from the driver's seat of the carriage.

"There it is, Sadie. We must stay together—especially if the ferry is crowded." Lucy tugged at Sadie's hand, and the pair headed toward the dock to board the ferry. After the arriving passengers had exited the vessel, the captain loaded trunks and bags onto the vessel. Sadie and Lucy joined about fifteen others taking the ferry across the river.

Gazing out at the surrounding marshes, Sadie breathed in the salty air and watched seagulls swooping down to locate fish in the tall reeds. Although the ride was fairly smooth, the chugging motions of the ferry made Sadie feel a tiny bit queasy. She drew in deep breaths and kept her gaze straight ahead, trying to focus on Lucy's chatter about what Aunt Matilda had planned for them.

To Sadie's relief, the ride wasn't a lengthy one, and before too long they were pulling up at the dock of the island to unload. Making sure not to mention her queasiness to Lucy, Sadie moistened her lips. Moments later the ill feelings passed, and Sadie lifted a silent prayer of thanks.

Despite the buzz of passenger voices and noise from the ferry, Sadie took in the peaceful view that greeted her. She admired the lush greenery abounding on the island, and the stately Live Oak trees draped in Spanish moss. An April breeze blew in from the ocean, offering a refreshing welcome.

"There's Aunt Matilda." Lucy exclaimed, tugging Sadie toward the middle-aged woman.

"Welcome, girls, I'm so glad you've arrived." Aunt Matilda threw her arms around her niece, then grinned at Sadie before bestowing a warm hug around her neck. "I'm so happy to finally meet Sadie. My, my, Lucy has spoken so highly of you, my dear." The look Matilda gave Sadie was filled with kindness. Sadie liked her right away.

"We must get your trunks, then Charles will drive us home in his carriage." At her niece's puzzled look, she explained. "He's a kind friend who lives on my road, and he's been so helpful to me." Matilda hurried toward the ferry to oversee the young women fetching their trunks.

Before Sadie and Lucy could retrieve them, a tall, older man with a neatly-trimmed beard rushed toward them.

"I'll assist them, Mrs. Matilda." He tipped his hat at Lucy's aunt, then at the young women. With no lack of strength despite his obvious age, the man named Charles reached out and grasped the trunks, then carried them to his waiting carriage parked at the road.

Lucy winked at Sadie and giggled. "What wonderful

service you have here, Aunt Matilda." The older woman blushed and grinned at her niece.

Was a romance looming for the older couple? Since Sadie knew nothing about this Charles fellow, she shouldn't even imagine the possibility. For all Sadie knew, he could be a married man, simply helping out a widowed neighbor.

They arrived a short time later at Matilda's modest tabby home, and Sadie immediately felt comfortable there. Along the front of the house was a row of windows, allowing plenty of sunlight to stream into the living room and kitchen. Matilda had lovely figurines placed at various settings—on a shelf, on two small end tables, and even on some of her windowsills.

Sadie stepped over to admire one of the figurines, and leaned in to get a closer look. Tiny flowers of purple, yellow, and red surrounded the bluebird statue. "How pretty this is, Aunt Matilda." She'd decided to make sure and use the name Lucy's aunt had insisted on being called.

"Why thank you, dear. That was a gift from a dear friend in Brunswick. She knows I appreciate birds and flowers— although I suppose I appreciate all aspects of nature." Matilda laughed, and it came out sounding jolly. No wonder Lucy adored her aunt so much. She was a very pleasant person to be around.

After unpacking their trunks and getting settled, Sadie and Lucy joined Matilda for cups of tea at the small round table in front of a window.

Matilda bubbled with enthusiasm as she shared her plans for their visit. "I don't want you to return home exhausted, but I would like for you both to enjoy some sights while here on this lovely island."

"We're eager to do whatever you have planned for us, aren't we, Sadie?" Lucy eyed Sadie with wide eyes and an expectant smile.

Sadie bobbed her head in agreement. "Oh yes, I'm eager to see and do whatever you suggest, Aunt Matilda."

The older woman beamed at her guests' response, then added more details about several activities and places of interest.

Sure enough, Aunt Matilda was true to her word. She accompanied the young women on carriage rides to view the St. Simon's lighthouse and other local scenery. Sadie was fascinated by the marshlands and flocks of egrets searching for fish in the water. Several times Charles stopped the carriage so his passengers could observe deer nibbling grass behind the tall oak trees. It was hard to believe that Sadie was so close to her home, because it almost felt as if she was in another land. Amazing what a change of scenery could do, she mused with contentment.

On Sunday morning the three women attended Aunt Matilda's church—a charming, small clapboard building nestled among the trees and Spanish moss. The lovely stained glass windows on either side of the building fascinated Sadie. She found herself gazing at them while listening to the pastor deliver a sermon from the book of Romans in the Bible. A peace washed over her and Sadie was thankful Matilda had invited them to attend the worship service.

After the service ended, members of the congregation clustered in front of the building, visiting and laughing. Sadie was amused at how proudly she and Lucy were introduced to Matilda's friends. It was obvious Lucy's aunt was thrilled to be hosting visitors.

A tall, well-dressed man appearing to be in his early thirties approached them with halting steps. Before he reached them, Matilda bustled over to him, grabbing the man by his arm.

"Matthew. How wonderful to see you this morning. I want you to meet my special guests from Riverview. My niece, Lucy, and her dear friend, Sadie." Aunt Matilda took a step back and beamed, as if displaying a prized treasure for someone to admire.

Matthew smiled and bowed politely to the women, while acknowledging them each with a warm greeting. His eyes seemed to linger a bit longer on Lucy. Was Matilda perhaps doing a bit of match-making?

"You must join us for our evening meal today, Matthew. I'm cooking a pot of soup, and I always prepare too much." Matilda chattered away, giving Matthew the directions to her home and the time to arrive. Sadie couldn't help noticing the look of delight on Lucy's face when she realized the handsome man would be joining them for a meal.

The women returned to Matilda's home in the carriage driven by Charles. Casually mentioning that Matthew Sims was a widower who'd moved to the island only months earlier, Matilda added, "I'm kind of like a mother to the young man, since his own family lives in the Atlanta area. He's such a kind man and is all alone here, so I'm glad he's attending my church." The twinkle in her eyes confirmed to Sadie what she was doing.

During the afternoon the three women rested before preparing the evening meal. Sadie noted with amusement that Lucy seemed to be a little bit nervous and was also wearing a nice dress and jewelry—all for a casual dinner at home.

The evening turned out to be pleasant, with conversation and laughter abounding. Sadie enjoyed watching the interaction between their guest and Lucy, and it was obvious Aunt Matilda was pleased.

As the young women helped Matilda clean the kitchen later that evening, Matilda beamed. "I think Matthew finds you fetching, Lucy dear. And the fact that you've both been widowed is something you have in common."

Lucy patted her aunt's arm and grinned. "I am glad you invited Matthew to our dinner this evening, Auntie. He seems like a nice gentleman." A blush colored Lucy's face and she turned her attention back to the dishes she was washing.

The last day of their visit Aunt Matilda and the young women visited a local market, and the older woman continued introducing her houseguests to everyone she knew. As Sadie drank in the sights around her, a tall man suddenly caught her eye. With a quick glance in his direction, Sadie realized she didn't know the man, and besides, he was with a woman who was most likely his wife.

So why should he capture her attention so easily? Sadie knew the answer. He reminded her of a certain man who'd rushed to her aid recently after she had tumbled from her bicycle. The man whose face continued to reappear in Sadie's mind at various times, to her puzzlement. Why should she be thinking of Shaun O'Leary? He was certainly handsome and had been kind to help her, but she basically knew nothing about him.

"Sadie, look at these flowers." Lucy's voice snapped Sadie back to the present, and she turned to see the lovely bouquet her friend was holding—cheerful blooms of pink, purple, and yellow. "I think I'll get these for Aunt Matilda." Lucy whispered.

Silently chiding herself, Sadie knew she needed to keep her mind on what was going on around her, rather than daydreaming like a silly schoolgirl.

The next morning Charles drove them to the dock to board the ferry, and the mist hovering over the river matched Sadie's mood. Even though she'd be very happy to see Papa and her cats again, she couldn't deny feeling a wee bit sad at leaving the lovely island. Aunt Matilda had been the perfect hostess, and as she hugged Sadie the older woman insisted Sadie visit her again.

She noted that Lucy wasn't nearly as talkative as she'd been on the voyage over to the island. Did she too feel saddened at leaving the beautiful place? Or perhaps Lucy's mind was on the nice widower she'd met at her aunt's church.

The wind picked up, making the ferry ride even rougher.

Sadie regretted eating her breakfast quickly that morning, because now her stomach churned. In fact, she was becoming more queasy by the minute. Not wanting to alarm her friend, Sadie didn't mention her physical feelings, but kept her gaze focused straight ahead and tried to draw in slow, deep breaths.

Lucy looked at her and gasped. "Sadie, you look green. Are you sick?" Compassion and concern were evident in Lucy's voice, and she gently took hold of Sadie's hand and led her to a bench seat along one side of the ferry.

Willing herself to feel better, Sadie remained seated and very still until the ferry pulled up to the Brunswick shore. She sent up a silent prayer of thanks that despite her queasiness, she didn't lose the contents of her stomach. That would've been mortifying.

Lucy continued fretting over her until she saw her father's carriage ready to drive the women back to Riverview.

Once on firm land, Sadie drew in deep breaths of fresh air and felt a little better. She offered a shaky smile to Lucy. "I promise I'm fine now, Lucy. I ate my breakfast too quickly this morning, then being on the choppy waters didn't help. But thank you for looking after me."

Sitting at her own kitchen table with a cup of tea, Sadie had a disturbing thought. If she had become sick merely from taking a ferry ride across a river, how would she ever survive sailing across the ocean as a missionary?

~ ~ ~ ~

Restless. That April morning on his way to his office, his mind plagued him with doubts. Would the remainder of his life continue as it was now? Surely, he wouldn't live with his parents forever. No, after he'd accumulated a good amount of money, he would purchase his own place. *My own empty, lonely place,* the silent voice in his mind taunted him.

Although his marriage to Grace hadn't been perfect, at least he'd had a wife—someone to share a home and life with. Then after seeing her struggle with the typhoid and grow weaker by the day, how could he ever allow himself to love again? It had wrenched his heart in two to see an already-frail woman gradually deteriorate until death claimed her.

No, I refuse to dampen my spirits by reliving that time in my life. Shaun knew it accomplished nothing to think back on those days of Grace's illness and her death. Not to mention the melancholy days following her funeral and burial.

Other memories almost as painful resurfaced now—the nights of attempting to numb his pain and lonely existence by visiting Savannah's taverns. That had been a huge mistake, which he still regretted.

It was most likely for the best that he was scheduled to take the train from Savannah to Riverview the next day. At least he'd have a change of scenery—not to mention a chance at seeing a certain lady in the town.

"G'morning, Mr. O'Leary. How are ye, today?" Cyrus MacDougal, one of his father's most faithful, hard-working employees greeted Shaun as he entered the building near the Savannah port. The Scottish man's friendly tone always gave Shaun a lift, and he'd often wondered if Mr. MacDougal truly possessed the temper Shaun had heard about.

"I'm well, Mr. MacDougal, and how are you, sir?" Shaun stood only a few feet from his office but paused to allow time for the older man to reply.

"Fairly well for an old man, and glad to still be kickin'." Mr. MacDougal gave a hearty laugh, to which Shaun joined in.

George O'Leary called out before Shaun had a chance to get settled at his desk.

"Good morning, Father. I'm all set to travel to Riverview in the morning and will hopefully return with some encouraging news. I'm also planning on getting a room there so I can stay close by as I supervise the project." Shaun surprised himself with the confident tone of his words. What if he was still unable to persuade the banker to assist him in purchasing the property in Riverview? He'd feel like a fool returning to his father bearing that news. So he shoved the negative thoughts from his mind and spoke with George O'Leary about other business-related matters.

As Shaun was about to return to his own desk, his father stopped him. "Shaun, be certain to let your mother know whenever you will be out of town for a few days. Although you're a grown man, your mother tends to fret about you if she doesn't know your whereabouts, and that fretting only brings on more headaches." His father's tone was sincere, but Shaun had the feeling George O'Leary was holding back a roll of his eyes.

~ ~ ~ ~

Traveling by train had never been Shaun's preferred mode of transportation, but sometimes it was necessary. Looking out his window at the passing scenes, Shaun's mind had already arrived at his destination. He'd have to keep the goal of his trip first and foremost, of course. Shaun was there to handle an extremely important business deal for his father, and this time he must return home to Savannah with more encouraging news. He was still surprised his father hadn't been more upset after Shaun's previous trip to Riverview, but George had handled that situation much better than expected.

However, this was Shaun's second attempt to find out who owned the piece of land his father wanted the company to purchase, so he must be productive with his time, whether or not he encountered a certain woman.

The rocking motion of the train lulled Shaun into a light slumber, but soon enough the conductor hollered out,

"Riverview. Next stop Riverview."

Shaun sat up straighter. It was time to focus on the real reason he was in the small town again. After reaching for his satchel, he checked his watch. Right on schedule, pretty much. He hoped the banker would be prompt for their meeting, but more importantly Shaun hoped the man would be receptive and offer the necessary information.

Only a handful of other passengers disembarked the train along with Shaun. He quickened his step so as not to be in the path of smoke when the train pulled away. The April sun shone down on him. What he wouldn't do for a drink. Taking another quick look at his watch, he felt certain he'd have time to visit the general store and purchase a cup of cider. Shaun could already imagine the cool liquid sliding down his parched throat, and he moistened his lips in anticipation.

Stepping into Hatcher's Store, Shaun immediately smelled the welcoming aromas of his previous visit—bread baking, chicory coffee, and assorted fresh produce on the counter near the door. It was interesting that the combined scents of such varied items would produce such a pleasing fragrance.

"Welcome, and come right in, sir. How can we help you today?" The same jolly, plump woman who'd helped him before now greeted him. A spark of recognition lit her blue eyes, and she smiled warmly. "Well, hello there, Mr. O'Leary. What brings you back to Riverview?"

"Hello ma'am. I'm here for a business appointment, but the train ride from Savannah made me thirsty. I want to purchase a cup of your delicious cider, please."

The storekeeper's wife looked more than a little pleased. She handed him the cup of cider, then took the coin from his hand and grinned. "Now if you finish that here and want another cup, it's on the house." Mrs. Hatcher ran her hands down the front of her apron, smoothing it, then turned her attention to straightening items on the counter near the cash register.

Perhaps it was due to being so thirsty, but that was the best cider he'd ever tasted. He actually did want a second cup, but intended on paying. Although it appeared the Hatchers had a thriving general store, they were by no means wealthy folks.

After insisting on giving payment, he accepted another cup of cider, drank it, then thanked Mrs. Hatcher. "I'm sure I'll be stopping in again before too long." He grinned at her, noting that rosy hue on her cheeks.

Feeling refreshed and ready to face the bank president, Shaun held his satchel with one hand and pushed the door with his other hand, nearly colliding with a beautiful young woman. A familiar-looking young woman. Sadie Perkins.

"I beg your pardon, ma'am. Are you all right?" Shaun was still holding the door handle but had stepped over to allow Sadie room to enter the store.

Her startled expression and gasp let Shaun know she must've been deep in thought.

"I'm sorry, Miss Perkins. I did not mean to almost knock you down." Shaun grinned, hoping to put her at ease.

She averted her eyes and clutched a small wicker basket close to her chest. "I'm fine, sir. No need to apologize—I had my mind on my shopping and wasn't thinking about anyone leaving the store."

"It is Miss Perkins, is that correct? Aren't you the lady I recently met up the road, after a small bicycle mishap?" Shaun didn't want to embarrass her further, but she hadn't said anything to indicate she recognized him.

Sadie winced. "Yes, that was me, I'm afraid. And you were more than kind to come to my aid that day, Mr. O'Leary." She lowered her eyes a moment, and dark eyelashes fluttered over a flawless complexion.

"Please, call me Shaun. And again, my apologies for almost causing you to take another tumble. Are you doing well?" The clock was ticking, and he must be on time to meet with the bank president. Shaun attempted to think of a polite way to ask if he could see her again, but his mind went blank. Besides, for all he knew Sadie Perkins could have a beau. What man wouldn't be taken with such a charming creature?

Sadie peered into the store and smiled. "It was nice to see you again. I hope you have a pleasant day." As she brushed past him into the store, a light scent of lavender drifted to Shaun's nose.

Shaun gently closed the door behind her and continued on his way, feeling a mixture of elation and frustration. Sure, he was thrilled to encounter the beautiful woman again, but why did it have to be when he was in a hurry? He'd have to think about her later, because at the moment he had an important meeting. And its outcome could depend on how well Shaun focused and conversed with the bank president.

~ ~ ~ ~

If Shaun wasn't so excited, the steady rhythm of the train might've lulled him to sleep on the way back to Savannah. But too much had happened, and thankfully it was all positive. He glanced down at his satchel that now contained important papers. He could hardly wait to show his father. George O'Leary would no doubt be proud his son had secured the purchase of the desired Riverview property for O'Leary Land Development Company.

Shaun had to admit that he was also happy he'd chanced to see the lovely Sadie Perkins again, although he'd almost knocked her down in the doorway of Hatcher's General Store. The image of her wide-eyed gaze, startled by his exit lingered in his mind. Even with a surprised look on her face, Sadie was still beautiful. Her emerald-green eyes and thick lashes seemed so...breathtaking. Yet in a soft, innocent way. Totally different from the women he used to encounter in the taverns.

A silent reminder that he still knew nothing about the woman niggled at Shaun, and he determined that the next time he was in Riverview, he would learn more about Sadie Perkins. Perhaps he would inquire of the storekeeper's wife, Mrs. Hatcher. Shaun felt certain the friendly, talkative woman would be a fount of helpful information, but he'd have to be careful how he obtained it. He couldn't simply blurt out a question asking if Sadie had a beau. He'd plan his approach on the next train ride to Riverview, but at the moment he was headed home to Savannah with his wonderful business-related news.

After departing the train station and taking a carriage to his parents' home, his stomach roared for food. Even if he had missed the evening meal, Maude always set aside some food for him. The very thought of one of Maude's sumptuous meals made his stomach rumble even more.

"Here you are, Mr. O'Leary." The carriage driver thanked him for the payment and generous tip.

Dusk was approaching and the crickets had begun their evening concert as Shaun headed to the front porch of the stately O'Leary home. Although it wasn't quite dark, lamps from inside the house offered a welcome glow.

After he entered, voices came from the dining room. He wasn't too late for dinner. "I'm home from Riverview," he called out so as not to startle anyone with a sudden appearance at the dining room door.

"Shaun, come join us, son. We're having our dessert now, but Maude can serve you a bowl of stew." Colleen spoke in a rather cheerful tone, which was a surprise to Shaun. She must not have one of her headaches.

Shaun propped his satchel against one wall. "Maude's stew smells delicious, so I'm glad there's some left. I haven't eaten in a while, and I'm famished." He grinned at the housekeeper, who was standing in the doorway that joined the kitchen and dining room.

"I'll be right there, Mister Shaun. You just get settled

and tell your family about your day." Maude scurried back into the kitchen to prepare his food.

George O'Leary took a sip of his coffee, then smiled at his son. "I trust your meeting with the bank president was productive this time?" He raised an eyebrow expectantly.

Trying to keep his excitement in check, Shaun returned a smile. "Yes, Father. Quite productive. I'll go ahead and say that I will be needing to rent a room at a Riverview boardinghouse now and then." That would sum up the fact that the hotel project would be able to begin in the near future. The details could be shared after he ate.

Shaun's mother gasped as she almost dropped her fork. "What?" She looked from Shaun to her husband in disbelief. Placing a hand to her bosom, she spoke in a distraught voice. "A child of mine will be staying in a boardinghouse?"

George gently patted his wife's arm and softly calmed her. "Colleen, I'll explain later. He means that he will be overseeing a project in that small town, so rather than make so many train trips between Savannah and Riverview, he'll stay there. It's only temporary, I promise you." He again patted his wife's arm.

Thankful when his mother appeared relieved, Shaun eyed the bowl of warm stew Maude had placed in front of him, along with a small plate of cornbread slathered in butter. He had to resist the urge to scoop up the chunks of beef and potatoes and shovel them into his mouth, because his hunger had intensified with its aroma.

As Shaun ate and his parents finished dessert and coffee, Maggie chattered happily about a young man who'd expressed interest in her. *Aha, that must be why my mother seems in good spirits.* Shaun had no doubts his mother would be happy to see Maggie with a beau in her life.

But how would Colleen O'Leary feel about someone like Sadie Perkins? A young woman from a small town who most likely was not from a wealthy family of socialites. Did it even matter? Although he'd always tried to please his parents, where matters of the heart were concerned, it should be his choice—and his alone.

Chapter Three

"That can't be true, Lucy. It just can't be." Sadie shook her head in disbelief after hearing her friend's words. The two women sat at the kitchen table in Sadie's home, sharing tea and gingerbread cookies Sadie had baked.

Lucy's eyes widened and she took a quick sip of her drink, then dabbed at her mouth. "I was shocked too. But Mrs. Hatcher said she heard it from a reliable source. The proposed hotel will be built on the land on Willow Lane, and that lovely house will be torn down." Lucy frowned. "It seems like such a horrible waste to destroy something so beautiful. Although it certainly could use some repairs, it's still a good structure. And that property has all those nice trees—it's always reminded me of a park, in a way. Such a peaceful place." Lucy released a sigh, then reached for another gingerbread cookie.

Sadie no longer had an appetite for her favorite treat. She sat, staring numbly at her friend across the table. It was as though she'd just been given terrible news of a loved one's illness or a tragedy that had happened. *No, this cannot be true. There must be a mistake.*

To her dismay, a lump had formed in her throat. "I know I've shared this with you before, but that house is so special to me because of the walks my mother and I took on that street years ago." Sadie paused, drawing in a deep breath to steel herself before continuing. "My mother always told me that maybe one day I could live in that house. Even though I've never expected to live there—or even in a house that large—it's still been a symbol of a dream to me." Forcing out a chuckle, Sadie shrugged. "I guess that sounds silly to you."

Lucy reached across the table and patted her friend's hand. "No, it doesn't sound silly at all. We've all got dreams of some kind, and that one is very sweet—especially since it goes back to the days when you took walks with your mother." An understanding smile formed on her lips.

The two friends sat in silence for a few moments, then Lucy brightened. "Now, tell me about your missionary plans. Have you done any more research or learned any new information? I don't want to hear news about my best friend from Dolly Hatcher, bless her heart." Lucy giggled and covered her mouth.

Sadie smiled, thankful her friend was interested in her plans. "I don't have any new information. I've been praying for the Lord to show me what to do and where I need to serve Him. But I'm leaning more toward Africa. The thoughts of traveling there and helping orphans thrills my heart." Sadie clasped her hands together and placed them under her chin. "I definitely feel called to do something with young children, because that's where my heart is."

"I'm not surprised to hear you say that, Sadie. You have a special way with children. I've observed you when you're reading to the children at the library. You love them, and they love you. I also agree you need to do some type of mission work involving young children. If that's where the Lord leads, of course."

The women visited a little while longer, then Lucy returned to the home she shared with her parents, clasping a small package of gingerbread cookies Sadie sent with her.

As she prepared supper for herself and Papa, Sadie thought back on her conversation with Lucy. She wouldn't let herself think about the beautiful house being torn down. No, instead she'd focus on preparing for the mission field. After all, she had been praying about it for quite a while and felt she was truly being called to serve.

If only her heart wasn't heavy about leaving Riverview. Being so far away from Papa, Lucy, and all her special friends in the small town that was home would be a challenge.

A weight seemed to perch on her shoulders. She shook her head in an attempt to clear it, knowing it was wrong to allow worries to take over. As a Christian, she must trust the Lord. If He did indeed want her to be a missionary in Africa, then He would give her the strength and courage she needed. One of Sadie's favorite verses from the Bible echoed in her mind.

I will instruct thee and teach thee in the way which thou shalt go. The familiar verse from the book of Psalms replayed over and over, until a gentle peace washed over her. If only she would keep that verse in her mind and trust in the Lord's guidance, then perhaps the worries and fears wouldn't overtake her as they had moments earlier.

~ ~ ~ ~

"Sadie, dear. How are you today?" Dolly Hatcher's greeting accompanied her usual welcoming smile as she tidied the counter of the store.

"I'm well, thank you Mrs. Hatcher. How are you and Mr. Hatcher doing?" Sadie smiled, removing the shopping list from her reticule. She wanted to be polite but was eager to complete her shopping and enjoy the lovely April day.

"Oh, we're doing fair to middlin', I suppose. Especially for folks our age." Dolly cackled, then her expression sobered a bit. "But Fred and I are gettin' more curious by the day about the big fancy hotel our town is supposed to be getting." She paused and shook her head.

"I'm not sure if we should be excited about it or worried. Riverview is such a peaceful little town, and the thought of hosts of tourists coming in and staying here for a while makes me a mite concerned." Her brow furrowed in a frown, and she clamped her lips together as if afraid she'd said too much.

"Do you know any details regarding the location of the hotel? I had heard it was to be built not far from the river but wasn't sure if a specific location had been determined yet." Sadie clasped her basket, glad it was empty and not yet heavy.

Dolly's eyes brightened and she moistened her lips, as if preparing to give a speech. "Well, from what I've heard, the land developer wants to buy the property on Willow Lane. That lovely piece of land with the big house on it. What a shame no one has lived there for a while—ever since the Martin family moved away." A shadow flitted over her face, then her bright countenance returned and she continued, "Anyway, from what I've been told by a reputable source, that's where the resort hotel is to be built. It shall be interesting to see if it actually occurs, and how it affects our town."

Sadie shook her head. "I'm sorry to hear that the particular piece of land you mentioned is where the hotel will be built. That's such a lovely house, with all those trees surrounding it. Do you really think that property is large enough to accommodate a hotel?" Although Dolly Hatcher had no impact on the decision at all, she was still curious as to what the woman thought, other than the fact she didn't want a large number of out-of-town folks swarming into Riverview.

A customer stepped to the counter at that moment, so Dolly hurried to take her place at the cash register. But she glanced at Sadie, offered a small smile, and shrugged. "I don't know, dear. I suppose we'll have to wait and see." The storekeeper turned her full attention to the female customer while she rang up the woman's groceries.

As Sadie went about her shopping, Dolly's voice chattered away about the weather, the fruits and vegetables the store would be offering the coming month, and Mr. Hatcher's arthritis acting up.

Sadie and Dolly weren't able to discuss the hotel or the land on Willow Lane anymore that day, because more customers entered the store, and Fred Hatcher was the one who rang up Sadie's groceries. Which was just as well, Sadie told herself. Because dwelling on thoughts of that beautiful house—her dream house—being torn down and replaced by a hotel caused her heart to sink. It didn't matter that she silently chided herself and tried to focus on thoughts of becoming a missionary. That cloud of sadness hung over her. She had much more praying to do.

Securing the small basket onto her bicycle handlebars, she tried to push away what Dolly Hatcher had shared. But now it seemed that the house and land on Willow Lane would be the site of the new hotel.

Releasing a sigh, Sadie determined to enjoy the lovely day and not be downcast from what she'd learned. She climbed onto her bicycle, her gaze traveling to the other businesses on Riverview's main street. A man was coming out of the bank. A familiar-looking man. He hadn't noticed her, but was now heading in the opposite direction toward the train depot.

With her heart pounding faster, she recognized him. *Shaun O'Leary.* But why would he be doing business in the Riverview bank, since he lived in Savannah? Well, perhaps it had something to do with the company he worked for, and besides—what did it matter to her?

~ ~ ~ ~

"Shaun, it's five o'clock and I'm heading home. Your mother has requested that Maude have our dinner prepared earlier from now on. It seems she thinks we've been dining too late and it's causing her stomach distress during the night." George shrugged. "Personally, I think your mother's stomach problems—as well as her headaches—stem from all her worrying."

Resisting the urge to comment on the fact his mother didn't have a care in the world, Shaun remained silent at his father's comment. Then he smiled as he stood from his desk. "Okay, Father, I'll be along soon myself. I have a few more figures to look over regarding the lumber shipments, then I'll hail a carriage and return home." Shaun stretched his back muscles before resuming his seated position at his desk.

After George O'Leary exited the office building, the area was quiet—with the exception of distant voices and the clopping of horses' hooves on the street. Shaun was eager to finish his day's tasks and head home. Not that anything special was awaiting him at his parents' home, but at least then Shaun could be alone with his thoughts about a certain woman he wanted to see. He only wished he knew when he might see her again.

His one-day trip to Riverview the previous day had only been to sign some papers and discuss details with the bank president. It wasn't surprising that Shaun hadn't even come close to catching a glimpse of Sadie. Hopefully, once he was there for longer periods of time overseeing the hotel project, that would change.

At the dinner table that evening, Maggie chattered on about her job at the bank, as Shaun's parents nodded at their daughter's comments. Shaun listened with half an ear at his sister's ramblings about bank patrons and fellow employees. Then Maggie mentioned a young woman who had her eye on Shaun.

"Yes, Shaun, she's pretty and nice and only a little younger than you. She comes into the bank about once a week—usually with her father. We visit quite a bit, and she's made comments about my brother. So that tells me she's interested in you. I'll be happy to find out more information about her, if you'd like." Maggie grinned at Shaun and twirled her hair with a finger.

Shaun cringed at his sister's comments. He loved Maggie, but at times like this she perturbed him. To his dismay, his parents had stopped eating and were watching him to see his response. *Why won't they leave my personal life alone? If I choose to court someone, then I'll decide. I don't need my family helping me in that area.* Bristling, he needed to be careful with his reply.

"Thank you, but I don't think I'm interested in your friend at the moment. But should I change my mind, you'll be the first to know." He forced a teasing wink at his sister, then resumed his eating. To his relief, his parents didn't comment. Most of all Shaun was relieved that Maggie's topic of conversation had not led to his mother once again mentioning the eligible Savannah debutantes. Shaun might scream if he heard much more about Savannah's single women from wealthy families.

His family meant well, but there was only one woman on his mind these days. And that woman most likely wouldn't be considered suitable by his parents—or at least by his mother.

Without a doubt Sadie Perkins had captured not only Shaun's eye but was tugging at his heart too. If he could only spend more time with her, then perhaps he'd have a chance to court her. That is, if she felt the way he did.

The next day, Shaun was handling an errand when he heard a male voice call to him. "Hey, O'Leary, where've you been? The boys and I haven't seen you at Riley's in a while." The burly-looking man grinned at Shaun from the doorway of the Savannah bank.

Shaun offered a smile and shook his head. "Hello, Maxwell. No, I've tried to stay away from the taverns. I was waking up with too many headaches. Any news?"

"Nah, just the usual work at the Savannah port. But remember ol' Norton? He's finally gettin' hitched. Can you believe it? Seth Norton settling down and getting married. Me and the boys told him we'll miss him at the tavern." Maxwell burst into raucous laughter, causing several bank patrons to glance his way.

Shaun chuckled and commented that he was happy for their mutual acquaintance, then eased out the door of the bank. Sure, Jed Maxwell had been one of his friends, but Shaun had tried to distance himself from the man and the others who were regulars at the local taverns. Not that he felt he was any better than those men, but he no longer had any interest in whiling away his evening hours in a local tavern. Especially since numbing his grief with alcohol had only left him more miserable.

Heading back to his office, he pondered the small bit of news Maxwell had shared. Another acquaintance, Seth Norton, was getting married. Not that Shaun was overly surprised, but he had an unsettled feeling. After a moment it hit him. Was he wishing it was him getting married again? After Grace had died, Shaun had vowed for a while that he'd never remarry. He didn't think he could bear to go through that kind of grief again, not to mention feeling angry at God for allowing his precious wife to be taken from him.

Although Shaun's feelings toward God hadn't softened completely, his thoughts regarding marriage had changed. Could it have something to do with meeting Sadie Perkins? What was it about her that drew Shaun so? It was more than her pretty face and sweet nature. Whatever it was, Shaun knew he wouldn't be at peace until he had the chance to get to know her better. Would that ever happen? Or was Shaun O'Leary destined to be a single man the remainder of his life?

~ ~ ~ ~

"That was a fine sermon today, wasn't it, Papa?" Sadie set their dinner on the kitchen table the following Sunday afternoon. The slices of beef, bowl of potatoes, and warm biscuits were all prepared, and Sadie giggled when her father patted his stomach and eyed the food with anticipation.

After Horace offered up a blessing for the meal, he nodded his head while placing a slice of beef onto his plate. "Yes, I agree. Pastor Lucas always does a superb job with his preaching, but today's message was extra good. And from what I saw, other folks thought so too. Lots of heads nodding in agreement with the pastor." Horace grabbed a biscuit and took a bite, obvious pleasure lighting up his weathered face.

Sadie decided to go ahead and share something on her heart with Papa. After all, he was in a very pleasant mood at the moment, enjoying the meal she'd prepared. "Papa, I spoke to Pastor Lucas as I was leaving the building this morning. You were talking with the Morgans and Doc Wilson, so I knew you didn't hear me. But I asked the pastor if he would have time for me to visit one day and discuss my—" Sadie's voice trailed off and she swallowed. Why was she having such a difficult time verbalizing this to her father? After all, he knew his daughter had been praying about doing mission work.

Seeing that her father had stopped eating and was gazing curiously at her across the table, Sadie needed to keep her voice casual. "My mission work." Sadie finished her sentence, then grabbed her cup of tea and took a sip.

Her father looked thoughtful, then slowly spooned more potatoes onto his plate. "So…Sadie girl. You're still thinkin' about doing mission work? It wasn't just a passin' fancy?" He resumed eating but kept glancing at his daughter between bites, interested in her comments.

"Yes, Papa. I'm still praying about serving the Lord in the mission field, and I'm serious about it. So no, it's not just a passing fancy. But what do you think, Papa? Even though I want to do the Lord's will, I also care about how you feel. I'd never want to do anything that wasn't pleasing to you." To her dismay, tears formed, and she blinked them away. She must stay strong, or she'd alarm her father. And besides that, how on earth would she survive serving as a missionary if she couldn't even discuss the topic with her own father without becoming emotional? Sadie chided herself as she hopped up from the table to take butter from the icebox. She hoped her father hadn't noticed the moisture pooling in her eyes.

She pasted a smile on her face and returned to her seat. To her relief her father was looking at his plate and eating, rather than gazing at her. Sadie attempted to eat a little more, but she wasn't hungry any longer.

After wiping his mouth, Horace peered at Sadie. He wasn't smiling, but didn't appear overly concerned either. "Well, as I've mentioned to you before, if serving the Lord in mission work is where you feel called, then that's what you need to do. You know I'd sure miss you if you was to be called to another land. But I'm not goin' to argue with the Lord, because He knows what's best. So you keep prayin' about it and I will too."

Feeling emotional once again, Sadie nodded and picked up her cup of tea. A soft meow came from the floor, and Sadie glanced down. Moses sat in the middle of the kitchen, looking up at her with his green eyes.

Sadie and her father both laughed, then Horace shook his head. "I think Moses is tellin' you that since we've eaten, it's time to feed your cats."

Thankful for the diversion, Sadie rose from her chair to place some scraps of meat on a saucer for her felines. She was secretly relieved the talk about her mission work was finished for now. But she did have the peace in knowing her father approved if that was what Sadie was called to do.

As she washed dishes, her mind returned to the previous week. She thought back to seeing Shaun O'Leary leaving the Riverview Bank, and it still puzzled her. Although Sadie told herself it didn't matter, she was overcome with curiosity as to why a Savannah man would be doing business there in Riverview.

But more importantly, Sadie couldn't deny her growing attraction to the man. If she was honest with herself, Shaun O'Leary was a man she'd like to know better—really know his personality, his likes and dislikes.

A thought seemed to hit Sadie square in the face, and she blew out a long sigh. Even if she did get to know the man better, what would it matter? If she was going into the mission field, what was the likelihood of a relationship developing between them?

~ ~ ~ ~

The next day dawned sunny and pleasant—the perfect day to garden. Sadie's father had prepared the small patch on the west side of their cottage, and although the coastal soil wasn't always ideal for what she wanted to grow, Sadie delighted in her small garden of bean plants, zinnias, and marigolds. It always amazed her how quickly the weeds overtook her small plot, but Sadie always felt a sense of accomplishment after pulling the stubborn strands from the ground, leaving only the growing plants.

Kneeling in the dirt with the morning sun on her back, Sadie was thankful the heat and humidity of summer hadn't yet arrived. Moses and Levi sprawled nearby, overseeing their owner's work. Their soft fur gleamed in the sun's rays.

"Sadie," A familiar voice called out, startling the cats and causing Sadie to jerk her head up from her task.

Lucy lifted the hem of her dress as she came hurrying

towards Sadie.

"Good morning, Lucy. What are you doing out and about this morning?" Sadie stood from the ground and brushed pieces of dirt from her calico skirt. She was more than a little curious as she noticed Lucy's flushed face and a sparkle in her eyes.

"Oh Sadie, I'm sorry to interrupt your gardening work, but I simply had to come and tell you my latest news. Remember Matthew from St. Simon's Island? Well of course you do—that was a silly question." Lucy giggled at her own comment before continuing. "He's coming to Riverview for a visit, Sadie. Isn't that wonderful?" Lucy clasped her dainty hands together underneath her chin and batted her eyelashes. She appeared more excited than Sadie remembered seeing her before.

After making certain she had no dirt lingering on her hands, Sadie reached over and gently squeezed her friend's hands. "Lucy, that *is* wonderful news, and I want to hear every detail. Do you have time for a cup of lemonade? I'm already eager to take a small break from my gardening."

The two women headed into the Perkins' cottage, with the two cats sauntering behind them. The aroma of that morning's coffee lingered in the air, creating a pleasant welcome as the women entered the kitchen.

Lucy shared the details of Matthew's upcoming visit, her excitement infectious. It was obvious the widow was bubbling with happiness.

Later that day while Sadie prepared the evening meal, she replayed what Lucy had shared with her. It was no secret that the vivacious widow was more than ready to marry again, so Sadie often prayed that if it was the Lord's will, the proper gentleman would come into Lucy's life. Perhaps Matthew would be the one, and how thrilled Lucy would be. Sadie was genuinely happy for her best friend and was determined they'd stay in touch.

An unwanted yearning tugged at her heart, but Sadie

attempted to ignore it as she continued chopping potatoes and carrots. But she couldn't deny that longing that would not completely go away—her original dream of marrying and having children. And even living in the house on Willow Lane, if possible.

Sadie almost laughed aloud at her thoughts. Who was she kidding? She was not meant to marry or be a mother if her calling was to the mission field. Serving as a missionary would fulfill her desire to nurture and care for children, wouldn't it?

Before going to bed that night, Sadie opened her Bible to the book of Psalms, one of her very favorite books. Without giving it much thought, she turned to the verse in chapter thirty-two, and read the words softly. *I will instruct thee and teach thee in the way which thou shalt go.*

Sadie had read that verse countless times and believed it, but for the first time she saw the words with a deeper understanding. If she kept praying and seeking the Lord's will for her life, He would surely show her what she's supposed to do. And whatever it was, that would be the best for her, because the Lord never made a mistake.

Her only struggle was handling the longing of her former dream that stayed buried in the recesses of her heart. Yet Sadie knew with the Lord's help, she could get past that dream.

She plumped her goose-feather pillow and released a sigh. Oh, why couldn't life be simple as it was when she was a child? When Sadie and her mother took walks together and talked about the flowers and birds they saw. That memory only served to stir up another memory—walking past the house on Willow Lane and dreaming of someday living there with her very own family. Sadie had a feeling she'd be lying awake for a while that night.

~ ~ ~ ~

"How long will you be away, Shaun?" Colleen O'Leary stood in the hallway, hand poised on the oak banister as though needing the support. Her face held a mixture of concern and pain.

"Only a matter of days, Mother. I want to oversee the hotel project, and I'll need to meet with the architect and once the actual building process commences, I want to keep a close watch on the progress. So I'll stay a few days at a time, I am thinking." Shaun hoped his mother wouldn't make an ordeal out of his staying at the boardinghouse in Riverview. He was, after all, twenty-seven years old and not a lad needing his mother's supervision or approval.

Anticipating his mother's next question, Shaun would put her mind at ease. "I've already located a nice boardinghouse in Riverview, so I plan to lodge there. I assure you I will be fine, Mother. And as I've already said, it's only for a few days at a time. This project is important—both to Father and to me." He was ready to be on the way and didn't want to miss his train.

To Shaun's relief, his mother forced a smile, told him to be safe, and placed a quick peck on his cheek.

He boarded the train just in time, making a mental note to leave the house earlier next time. Settling into his seat, Shaun glanced around and was glad that this train wasn't overly crowded. He even had an empty seat beside him, so he placed his bag and satchel there.

As the train chugged along the tracks toward Riverview, Shaun's mind seemed to chug along too—with an abundance of thoughts going round and round. He couldn't deny feeling a surge of excitement at being able to oversee such an important project for his father's company, and also not being confined to a desk for days on end. He tended to feel restless when he remained in the office for an extended length of time.

But there was another reason for his excitement, and he hoped it wouldn't lead to disappointment. Would he be able to see Sadie Perkins and perhaps even learn more about her? That was his plan, and he was determined to give it his best try.

As Shaun stepped off the train onto the platform, a breeze stirred the air around him. The late April sky was clouding, and Shaun hoped rain would hold off at least until he'd secured a room at the boardinghouse and then visited the general store. It was funny, because even though he'd only visited the cozy town a few times, he felt comfortable here. Although he'd been happy living in Savannah, there was just something charming about the much-smaller town. The fact that it was located on the banks of the great Altamaha River appealed to Shaun, too. He was always happiest when he was near water.

Gripping his satchel in one hand and his heavier duffel bag in the other, Shaun headed in the direction of the boarding house he'd noticed on his last visit. Hopefully there would be an available room for him because he didn't have an alternative plan lined up.

The two-story clapboard house was nothing fancy but appeared to be clean and well-kept. Someone had planted orange and yellow flowers in beds along either side of the walkway leading to the porch. Shaun appreciated the colorful welcome and already had a good feeling in his gut about this place.

Since a small sign on the front door instructed visitors to ring the bell, Shaun did and immediately heard footsteps approaching. The door swung open, and an older woman greeted him with a cautious smile.

"May I help you, sir?" The woman had gray hair pulled up in a tight bun. Her dress was simple but neat.

"Yes, ma'am. I'll be staying in Riverview off and on for the next few months and wondered if you have an available room? My name is Shaun O'Leary and I'm from Savannah." He offered a smile, hoping to convince the woman he was a decent fellow.

She stepped back and gestured him into the front room of her house. "Yes, Mr. O'Leary, you're in luck. I do have a room here on the first floor, and at the present time, you will also have a private washroom. I serve two meals each day but occasionally take Saturdays and Sundays off. But I allow my boarders plenty of advance notice if I'm not to be cooking on a particular weekend. And I expect my boarders to be courteous and notify me ahead of time if they're not to be present at a meal. It helps immensely as I'm planning the amount of food I need to prepare." She paused, giving him a chance to digest the information.

Shaun wasn't sure if the woman was finished speaking, so he said, "Yes, ma'am."

She stuck out her hand and said, "I'm Miss Callie, and if you're interested in renting, please know that payment is expected weekly. I also do not allow smoking or drinking on my premises, but you don't appear to be a rowdy sort."

Amused at the woman's comment, Shaun grinned and was thankful Miss Callie hadn't seen him in his former lifestyle when he frequented the Savannah taverns.

"No ma'am. I'm not rowdy, and when here in your house, I'll most likely be sleeping, eating, or reading." Now he was curious about the other tenants but figured he'd find out what they were like in time.

Miss Callie showed Shaun to his room, which wasn't bad at all. It appeared the wallpaper had recently been redone, and there was even a small vase of flowers on the pine chest of drawers. A window adorned with checked curtains looked out over the front yard of the house, and Shaun was relieved. He didn't think he could bear to stay in a room with no windows.

"This appears quite nice, Miss Callie, and I do appreciate your allowing me to lodge in your house." Shaun set down his satchel and bag, longing to stretch out on the bed for a nap but knowing he had work to do.

"Supper will be served promptly at six o'clock, Mr.

O'Leary. You're not required to eat meals here, of course. However, as I've mentioned, I appreciate a notice if one is to be absent from a meal. But I've been told I'm a pretty decent cook." She grinned and left the room, footsteps echoing on the hardwood floors.

Shaun called out his thanks after her, then sat on the edge of the bed to collect his thoughts. *Focus, O'Leary. Remember why you're in this town. Not to pursue a woman, but to do a job and do it well.* Shaun's mental talk was a reminder that he had a major task ahead of him overseeing the hotel project, and that must be his primary focus.

He took paper and pen from his satchel and jotted down what he must accomplish in the next few days. Then he glanced at his watch. The hour was later than he'd thought. Thankfully his appointment with the banker wasn't until the next morning, but he did need to visit the land and have an idea about the hotel's placement before meeting with the architect. He'd do that and then return in time for Miss Callie's evening meal at six.

As Shaun walked the three streets over to Willow Lane, he took in the sights around him, feeling even more drawn to the town. Turning along the sidewalk to head toward the newly-purchased property, Shaun noticed a woman ahead of him, slowly climbing off her bicycle. She appeared to be staring at the house, sitting on the property surrounded by trees.

As a breeze stirred and the woman smoothed her chestnut mane of hair away from her face, Shaun realized her identity. *Sadie Perkins.* The same beautiful woman who'd inhabited so many of his thoughts lately, and now here she was, twenty feet ahead of him.

He didn't want to startle her, so he slowed his steps and continued observing her as she stared at the house. Had she lived there at one time? Shaun couldn't help wondering. Or perhaps she was simply out for a bicycle ride and had pedaled down Willow Lane, stopping to take a break.

As if sensing she wasn't alone, Sadie turned her head to the right and saw Shaun.

He increased his walking speed, smiling at her as he drew closer. "Hello there, Miss Perkins. I hope I didn't startle you."

"Mr. O'Leary, I'm surprised to see you here. Don't you live in Savannah?" A rosy hue crept up her face and the hint of a smile touched her lips.

"Yes, ma'am, but I'll be staying in Riverview on business. The boardinghouse where I'm lodging serves a meal at six o'clock, and I wanted to get some fresh air before eating. Of course I needed to stretch my legs, also, after the train ride from Savannah earlier today." He was being truthful with her, but didn't think this was the time to mention the hotel project on the very piece of land she'd been gazing at a minute earlier.

Understanding seemed to creep in, and her smile widened. "Are you staying at Miss Callie's house? She's a wonderful cook so you'll enjoy some delicious meals if you are."

Shaun grinned, trying not to think about the loveliness of the creature standing a mere two feet from him. "Yes, I'm staying there, and I'm glad to hear that her cooking is good. It appears I've made a wise choice in my lodging." He chuckled and was preparing to ask if she knew who used to live in the house, but she was ready to leave.

"It was nice seeing you again, and I hope your stay in Riverview will be pleasant. I need to be getting home to begin cooking for Papa. Good afternoon, Mr. O'Leary." With a polite smile, Sadie Perkins carefully climbed onto her bicycle and pedaled away from him.

Shaun stood as if frozen, watching her ride away. Had she been curious about his reason for walking along Willow Lane? Sadie accepted his statements about getting fresh air and stretching his legs.

How would Sadie feel about the proposed hotel in

Riverview? find out in time. At the moment, he was elated he'd encountered the woman again.

The clip-clop of horse hooves snapped Shaun out of his private thoughts, and he looked up to see a carriage driving past him. The family inside the carriage smiled and the children waved. Yes, Riverview was certainly a friendly town, and Shaun only hoped the friendly feelings would carry over into the reactions about the hotel.

He stepped onto the property, mentally making notes about the approximate location of the main building and the added features he and his father had discussed. To his surprise it was more difficult to visualize the hotel building as he viewed the two-story house standing before him. Shaun could tell that at one time the house had been beautiful, but apparently the most recent owners had not kept up the maintenance on it, and now much work would be needed to restore the building.

Shaun shook his head as if to clear those thoughts away. Why was he even thinking about the house? It would be completely torn down in a matter of weeks, if all went according to plan. When he glanced at his watch, Shaun was surprised to discover the time was almost six o'clock.

He needed to return to Miss Callie's to partake of the evening meal, and he didn't want to arrive late. Especially since this was his first evening at the boarding house. He wanted to maintain a good relationship with his landlady.

But as Shaun slowly walked back up Willow Lane away from the property, he had the urge to turn around and glance back at the house. Apparently that structure held some kind of special meaning for Sadie, or maybe she was simply pausing in her ride to view the house.

A distant rumble of thunder sounded, and Shaun quickened his steps. He was thankful the rain had held off so far, but he had a feeling a storm was approaching. At least he had a place to stay, so no need to worry about the weather.

As Shaun entered the boarding house, the aroma of fried

chicken wafted through the air, and his stomach growled in response. He had a feeling that after eating Miss Callie's meal, he'd sleep well that night. Shaun also had a feeling a certain beautiful woman named Sadie just might make an appearance in his dreams.

~ ~ ~ ~

"At least I didn't tumble off my bicycle this time." Sadie shrugged and shook her head. She and Lucy were visiting on the Perkins' porch the next day, and Sadie had told Lucy about stopping by the house on Willow Lane the day before.

With a slight giggle, Lucy patted her friend's arm. "Well, if you would've taken another fall, I'm sure that handsome gentleman would have gladly helped you again, Sadie. This sounds very romantic to me." Lucy clasped her hands beneath her chin and sighed.

Now it was Sadie's turn to giggle. "I don't really see anything romantic about falling from a bicycle, Lucy. But it was very kind of Shaun O'Leary to help me that day I fell."

Lucy nodded, then frowned. "Are you sure you've told me everything? You were on your way home from your library job, and you took a different route so you could look at that house you love. While you were looking at it, your rescuer just happened to come down the street. Are you certain you haven't left out anything?"

Sadie couldn't help laughing. "Lucy, you are a hopeless romantic, for certain. That was it, and no I haven't left out any details, I promise. You're my best friend, and you know I share everything with you." She was eager to get the attention off herself, so she changed the subject. "How about you tell me the latest information on Matthew?"

Happy to oblige, Lucy chattered about the upcoming visit of the widower from St. Simon's Island.

Sadie didn't miss the sparkle in Lucy's eyes as she spoke fondly of the man she'd only met the month before.

"Aunt Matilda is so happy we're keeping in touch. She says that we make a lovely couple—isn't that funny?" Lucy chuckled, her face turning crimson.

At the mention of Aunt Matilda, a thought crept into Sadie's mind. "What about Charles? The kind man who so patiently drove us in his carriage while we visited your aunt." Had she imagined the fond looks the older pair gave each other? Perhaps Charles and Aunt Matilda were only casual friends.

Lucy's eyes widened at hearing the mention of Charles. "He's such a kind man, but I think Aunt Matilda sees him more as a friend rather than a possible romantic interest. But I have to say he has been a wonderful friend for my aunt, and I feel better knowing Charles does things for her." Lucy hopped up from the wicker chair.

"Oh my, I really need to return home and help Mother with some chores in the house. After dear Edgar passed away, I was so thankful that my parents invited me to live with them again, so I do try and help Mother in the house." Lucy gathered her dress up so she wouldn't trip going down the steps from Sadie's porch.

As Sadie did the laundry that afternoon, her thoughts returned to the previous day when she'd stopped by the house on Willow Lane. *Her house.* Ha, she almost laughed aloud at that. It had only been her house in her dreams as a child during those walks with her precious mother. Now the rumor was the house would be torn down, and a hotel built on the property. *A hotel!* Why did Riverview need some fancy hotel? Sadie asked herself the question yet again, a tugging at her heart that she couldn't ignore.

Her only consolation was that if she did indeed leave to do mission work, she wouldn't be in Riverview when the house was demolished. Sadie didn't think she could bear to see that symbol of her dreams being torn down, even if it was for the supposed cause of progress.

Chapter Four

The rain that covered Riverview overnight had stopped, but now the morning air hung thick with humidity. Shaun left the boarding house after enjoying a delectable breakfast of eggs and bacon Miss Callie had prepared. After meeting the other boarders at the breakfast table, he found them pleasant enough and not the least bit rowdy.

He glanced at his watch and saw it was still fairly early, so he had plenty of time before meeting with the architect. Why did he feel a twinge of nervousness about this hotel project? The silent question echoed in his mind as he headed to the bank, the place they'd agreed to meet.

Deep down, he felt the strong urge to please his father. Handling this hotel project would be the perfect opportunity to show George O'Leary he was capable of being successful. Especially since Shaun had never felt he measured up to his father's expectations.

An unfamiliar man stood just outside the bank's doors, looking up and down the street. When he spotted Shaun, curiosity was evident in his face. "Mr. O'Leary? Are you Mr. Shaun O'Leary?" The man was now smiling and stepped toward Shaun.

"Yes, that's correct. I'm Shaun O'Leary." Shaun extended his right hand.

"I'm Elmer Louis Anderson, of Anderson Architects. Pleased to make your acquaintance." The stocky man with gray hair shook Shaun's hand.

Opening one of the doors, Mr. Anderson stepped back to allow Shaun entrance. As he followed behind, he explained. "The bank president, Mr. Withers, has graciously permitted us to use one of the rooms here in the bank. I thanked him profusely." The architect chuckled as though he'd made a joke.

Fighting nervousness, Shaun said, "I certainly appreciate your making these arrangements, Mr. Anderson."

"Please, call me Elmer," he spoke over his shoulder. He led the way into a small room at the rear of the first floor. "Thankfully this room has a window, so we don't feel like we're in a jail cell." The man again chuckled. He lowered his heavy frame into one of the four oak chairs in the room.

To Shaun's relief, the meeting went better than he'd expected. Elmer Anderson showed several plans he'd drawn up, discussing the advantages of each. He appeared to be interested in hearing Shaun's comments, which he appreciated.

When Shaun left the meeting over an hour later, he felt overwhelmed but excited. The Riverview hotel was becoming more and more of a reality. Just as important to Shaun, however, was the golden opportunity for him to finally prove himself to his father. This was his chance to show George that he could handle details and follow through with a major building project.

With his steps lighter as he exited the bank, Shaun decided to visit Hatcher's Store and pick up some food to eat in his room. Since Miss Callie didn't serve lunch, Shaun needed to keep some items on hand. Not to mention this might be his chance to learn more about Sadie, if he could get Mrs. Hatcher talking.

Shaun ignored the niggle of guilt at the thought of trying to learn more about the beautiful woman who'd captured his attention. After all, if he was going to pursue her, he needed to know more about her.

Stepping into the store, Shaun drew in a deep breath. As before, delightful aromas wafted through the air. He planned on purchasing some crackers and cheese along with some cider.

"Hello there, Mr. O'Leary. It's nice to see you again." Fred Hatcher came out from behind the front counter, smiling as he clutched a broom in one hand.

"Good afternoon, Mr. Hatcher. I've finished an appointment I had in town, and decided I needed to get something to eat before heading back to Miss Callie's." Shaun hoped the storekeeper didn't hear the rumbles coming from his middle.

"Well, you just let me know if I can be of help. And please, do call me Fred." The bald man began sweeping near the entrance.

Shaun couldn't resist a smile at the thought of the two men he'd spoken with that day—both insisting he call them by their first names. Yes, Riverview was definitely a friendly town.

Lifting a small package of crackers from a shelf, Shaun then went back to the front counter to ask for some slices of cheese and a small bottle of cider. Just as he stepped to the counter, Dolly Hatcher's voice reached his ears.

"Welcome, Mr. O'Leary. I'm glad to see you again. Is your business going well?" The plump woman brushed flour from her apron with one hand, and with the other tucked some loose hairs behind her ear.

After chatting for a few minutes and paying for his purchases, Shaun searched for a discreet way to bring Sadie into the conversation. To his dismay, nothing came to mind. He remembered she'd mentioned her job at the library.

Gathering his cheese, crackers, and cider, Shaun paused before walking toward the door. "I was wondering where the town's library is located. Since I enjoy reading, it would be a good way for me to spend the small amount of spare time I have while in town working." His pulse raced. Did she see right through his comments? After all, Shaun did enjoy reading, so he was being honest.

Dolly Hatcher informed him the library was located only two streets over, then she added, "And Miss Sadie Perkins works there three days each week, so if you visit on a day when she's there, I'm certain she'll be delighted to help you." Had Shaun imagined the mischievous twinkle in the woman's eyes?

Feeling his face heat up, Shaun thanked her and hastened out of the store. Yes, this might be the perfect way to learn more about Sadie without questioning the storekeeper's wife. He should've thought of this earlier.

Shaun hurried back to the boardinghouse, eager to eat his cheese and crackers. He was also eager to dwell on thoughts of a certain library worker, and only hoped she didn't have a beau.

~ ~ ~ ~

"Papa, I've decided I'll visit Pastor Lucas one day this week. After praying about it, I feel I need to go forward with more definite plans about mission work." Sadie attempted to keep her voice steady and casual, but she was certain her father noticed the slight nervousness in her words.

Even though Horace had assured Sadie she'd have his blessing, deep down her father would not want her to leave. And that tugged at her heart.

He had a faraway gaze in his eyes. "If that's what you feel called to do, Sadie girl, then you talk to the pastor. I would never stand in the way of what the Lord calls anybody to do." His voice was thick with emotion. He resumed eating, keeping his eyes lowered.

This might be harder than Sadie had thought. If simply talking about leaving to be a missionary caused such emotional feelings in Papa and herself, what on earth would happen when she actually boarded a ship to sail across the ocean?

She shoved the thoughts aside and changed the subject. "So tell me about the mill. How was work today?" Even though her appetite was gone, she still nibbled at her cornbread and beans.

Horace wiped his mouth and shrugged. "About the usual, except for the fellas talkin' about that fancy hotel our town is s'posed to get. I don't know what to make of all that, so I don't comment but just listen. It'll be interestin' to see what develops."

"Have you heard anyone mention the location of the new hotel, Papa?" Her pulse raced again as she thought of what Lucy had shared.

Frowning, Horace gazed across the table at her. "Well, I don't know if this is accurate or not, but a couple of fellas said it'll be somewhere on Willow Lane. But that could be just talk."

A sense of dread hung over Sadie. Hearing the location of the proposed hotel from more than one source seemed to indicate that Willow Lane would in fact be the location. And most likely the piece of land with the lovely home—*her* dream home—would be the site.

But what could she do? Launch a one-woman protest against the house being torn down and a hotel built in its place? No, of course not. She wanted to do something, but she had no idea what. So in the meantime, she would pray about it. *I'll add that concern to my prayers, in addition to praying about mission work.* She was thankful God was a good listener, because Sadie felt she was taking a lot of concerns to Him.

The next day she stayed busy at the library, placing

books on the shelves and assisting Polly White at the counter. Although she didn't mind those tasks, Sadie eagerly looked forward to having storytime with the children. A quick glance at the clock on the library wall showed that she only had thirty minutes until the children would be brought in, accompanied by their mothers.

As the library door opened and another patron entered, Sadie glanced up. She stifled a gasp. Shaun O'Leary.

The tall, well-dressed man stood at the door looking around. When his eyes met Sadie's, he smiled. After a pause, he walked toward her at the counter. "Hello, Miss Perkins. How are you today?" He spoke with a politeness, yet there was a playful glint in his eyes as he looked directly at her.

Sadie's heart raced and her breath seemed to turn into small gasps. What had gotten into her? Just because she wasn't expecting the attractive man to stop by the library was no reason to act like a love-struck schoolgirl.

Trying her best to remain calm and appear unaffected by his presence, Sadie smiled in return. "Hello, Mr. O'Leary. How nice to see you in our town's library. May I help you?" *Why wouldn't her hands stop trembling?* And to make matters worse, Polly White was eyeing them both curiously. She must wonder how Sadie knew this unfamiliar man.

Shaun now stood directly at the counter, a mere three feet from her. Still smiling, his voice and mannerisms exuded charm. "Thank you, but I had a bit of time and thought I'd stop in and look around. Since I like to read, I always enjoy visiting libraries."

The head librarian stepped over beside Sadie and introduced herself.

Shaun slightly bowed and continued smiling. "Pleased to meet you, Mrs. White. I'm Shaun O'Leary of Savannah, and am in Riverview on a business matter. I was just telling Miss Perkins how much I enjoy libraries and books."

Sadie didn't know if it was her imagination or not, but Polly White seemed to be fluttering her eyelashes and smoothing her hair. Fighting the urge to giggle, Sadie looked at the librarian. "Mr. O'Leary came to my aid recently when I took a tumble from my bicycle." Sadie felt herself blushing at the admission, and again thought of how foolish she must've looked that day.

Polly White and Shaun visited for a few minutes, and the librarian encouraged him to take his time browsing through the books.

"If there's something in particular you need, just let us know." Polly sent him a kind smile as a hint of pink colored her cheeks.

"Thank you, Mrs. White. I'll just look around before I need to be heading back. I've still got some more work to do before returning home to Savannah." He ambled toward the reference books and perused the shelves, lifting a volume now and then and flipping through it.

Sadie forced herself to focus on her work. The children would be arriving very soon, and she needed to prepare for story time. Sure enough, minutes later several mothers arrived with their children in tow. As soon as the children saw Sadie, they ran up to her, eager to know which book she'd chosen for that day.

As much as she'd been looking forward to reading to the children, Sadie was also a little disappointed that story time occurred while Shaun was visiting the library. She would've enjoyed talking with him a little more. But then it might have been awkward, so perhaps it was best that her young charges had arrived.

Leading the small group of children to a corner of the library, Sadie sat in her rocking chair as the youngsters huddled around her feet, eager faces peering up at her. Even though she tried to keep her focus on the children, Sadie couldn't help being aware of Shaun watching her.

Just as she began the story, she noticed Shaun glancing at his watch and then striding toward the door. But before going out, he caught her eye and smiled.

Although she felt a tiny bit let-down that the handsome man had gone, she also felt relief. Now she could completely relax and enjoy her time with the children.

Later that day as Sadie prepared to leave, Polly approached her, sporting a wide grin on her round face. "Oh my, Sadie. That visitor we had today was quite the handsome fellow. I have a feeling he stopped by to do more than peruse our books. He must certainly have an eye for you." Polly winked and gently squeezed Sadie's arm.

Taken aback, Sadie wasn't sure how to respond. This was completely out of character for the normally serious librarian. So she smiled and shook her head. "No, I think he truly enjoys books, as he said. But he does seem like a nice man." To her dismay she was certain her face was crimson.

Pedaling her bicycle home a few minutes later, Sadie reflected on Polly's comments. Had Shaun O'Leary stopped by to see her? The very thought made her heart race, and she gripped the handlebars. It was certainly not an unpleasant thought. In fact, if Sadie was honest with herself, she'd have to admit that she was flattered and thrilled.

~ ~ ~ ~

The next afternoon Sadie pedaled her bicycle to the home of Pastor Lucas. Although the coastal breeze had strengthened into a wind, Sadie was thankful for the sunshine streaming down. She hoped to appear calm and confident to her pastor, rather than nervous and windblown as she felt.

Mrs. Lucas greeted her at the door, the woman's plump face rosy and smiling. "Come right in, Sadie dear. Pastor is expecting you, but first I want to be sure and let you know that I've baked a butter cake and want to send some slices home with you. I do hope you and your father will enjoy it." The woman beamed proudly before leading Sadie to a small room in their house that served as the pastor's office. "When you finish your meeting, just let me know. I'll have the slices wrapped for you to carry in your bicycle basket."

Before Sadie could utter a thank you, Mrs. Lucas added. "I used my favorite recipe." She clasped her hands in front of her, pride glowing in her eyes.

The pastor's wife was known in Riverview for her tasty baked goods, so Sadie looked forward to enjoying the cake with her father.

"That's very kind of you, Mrs. Lucas. Thank you so much." Sadie returned a heartfelt smile, then stepped into the office to join the pastor.

Although Sadie had been nervous about what to say, once she began sharing her reasons for wanting to do mission work, she relaxed more.

Pastor Lucas nodded while she spoke, a serious but pleasant expression remained on his face. Sadie thought his wire-rimmed glasses gave him an intellectual appearance.

"I have no doubt you're sincere about feeling called. And I'm certain you do have a heart for children, which is evident when I've been in the library and chanced to see you reading to the youngsters." He cleared his throat and steepled his fingers, as though preparing to offer wise counsel.

A tense feeling crept over Sadie. Was Pastor Lucas going to tell her she was making a mistake? That there was no way she could be a missionary? The doubts tumbled through her mind as she waited for his advice.

"Now I am assuming you've been in prayer about this decision, Sadie. As I'm sure you realize, a life calling is not to be taken lightly, so I am also assuming you've talked with your father about this calling." The pastor smiled, as though offering reassurance.

Sadie sat up a little straighter in her chair, trying not to lean forward in her effort to emphasize that she'd done much praying and reading her Bible for discernment. "Oh, yes sir. I've prayed a lot and searched the Scriptures for guidance."

"Very good. I had a feeling you've been diligent with this, and you're wanting to do the Lord's will."

During the remainder of their conversation, Pastor Lucas offered suggestions of what Sadie needed to do next. He also spoke specifically of Africa, since Sadie had mentioned that was the country where she felt called.

Before leaving his office, the pastor assured Sadie he'd be in prayer also, and would be happy to assist her however possible. "I don't want to speak for members of our church, but I do feel that there are some in our congregation who would be willing to help with financial support, as that is an area that often hinders those desiring to be missionaries." He offered a kind smile and told her he would talk with her again soon.

Heading toward the door, Sadie remembered Mrs. Lucas mentioning the cake. Thankfully the woman was still in the kitchen and had the cake slices all wrapped. The sweet aroma from the baking cake lingered in the air.

"Here you are, Sadie dear. I do hope your meeting with Pastor went well, and please tell Horace to enjoy this cake. And you too, of course." She chuckled and patted Sadie's arm.

Sadie pedaled her bicycle more slowly on the ride home, being careful not to toss the wrapped cake out of her wicker basket. She could hardly wait to sample the treat, which she knew would be delicious.

A mixture of relief, joy, and fear all competed for her focus. She was thankful her meeting had gone well, and she was thrilled to have the support of Pastor Lucas. The fact he'd mentioned financial support from the church was also cause for relief. But fear took hold whenever Sadie allowed herself to think—*really* think—about sailing across the Atlantic Ocean to a foreign country. *It's not forever. Only for a while.* She hoped her silent talk would calm her unease, but Sadie knew the only remedy for her fears.

After she put away her bicycle and took the cake into the

kitchen to be enjoyed after supper, Sadie sat with her Bible opened in her lap. She read, over and over, one of her favorite verses in the book of Psalms. *I will instruct thee and teach thee in the way that thou shall go.*

Yes, if the Lord wanted her to be a missionary, He would show her exactly what to do. She must remember that, and not listen to her own fears and doubts.

~ ~ ~ ~

As Shaun rode the train back to Savannah, his thoughts were jumbled. He was eager to share the architect's ideas with his father, yet was overwhelmed at what lay ahead of him. Could Shaun handle all the responsibilities that went along with the hotel project? He had to handle the project, and not only handle it, but see it completed to George O'Leary's high standards.

He reached up and rubbed his temples as he felt a headache coming on. Apparently, he'd inherited his mother's tendency toward having frequent headaches—although he didn't use a hand on his forehead to gain sympathy. That thought almost made him grin, visualizing Colleen O'Leary's dramatic gestures.

Ignoring the headache pain while pushing all work-related thoughts from his mind, Shaun reflected on seeing Sadie Perkins. When he'd observed her at the library the day before, he again realized how beautiful she was. But there was something else about her too—a certain innocence and vulnerability. Not that he would think of her as being weak, because Shaun had a feeling that Sadie was the kind of person who would fiercely protect those she cared about. Yet there was a gentleness he'd noticed as she gathered the children around her so she could read a story to them.

She cared about children, so why wasn't Sadie married with children of her own? Perhaps he'd find out if and when he got to know her better. He earnestly hoped he would.

"Savannah, next stop!" The conductor's voice bellowed out, snapping Shaun from his thoughts of Sadie.

Once he arrived home, his father would await the information from his brief trip. That meant Shaun must focus and not allow his mind to wander to the lovely woman in Riverview.

After a carriage drove him from the train station to his parents' home, the sky grew darker. Not only from the impending dusk, but a storm must be brewing. He was arriving just in time.

"I hope you make it back before a storm begins." Shaun told the carriage driver as he paid and tipped the older man. Even the horses leading the carriage seemed to sense stormy weather was headed their way, their hooves pawing at the street.

The driver cast a worried glance toward the sky, then smiled at Shaun. "Thank you, sir. I hope so too. And in the event the storm begins while my horses and I are still out, the good Lord will keep us safe."

Shaun hurried up the sidewalk toward the front door, mulling over the carriage driver's words. Did the man actually believe what he'd said? When Grace had been ill, some of her family members had prayed for her—yet she still died from the typhoid. Shaun had grown bitter after that and wondered dozens of times where God had been. No, he wouldn't trust in anyone to keep him safe—or to prevent bad things from happening. Shaun knew better.

As he entered the house, Shaun drew in a deep breath, and the aromas from Maude's cooking wafted to his nose. Even though he was certain the family had finished their evening meal, Shaun hoped there was at least a bit of food remaining. His stomach was beginning to rumble, and he didn't want to wait until morning to eat.

Footsteps echoed in the hallway, and Shaun glanced up to see Maude.

"I thought I heard someone come in. Welcome home.

I'm guessing you haven't eaten, so have a seat at my little table in the corner. Unless you'd prefer to eat in the dining room." Maude winked at him before bustling around, gathering leftover food to heat on the stove.

"Your table is just right, Maude. And please don't go to trouble on my account. I could eat a slice of bread and some cheese from the icebox." Even though he was sincere, Shaun braced himself for the housekeeper's reply.

"Oh my! I would never let you scrounge for bread and cheese when I've cooked and there's plenty left." She playfully shook her head at him, then continued warming the food.

Minutes later, Shaun enjoyed a plate filled with Maude's sliced ham and potato salad as she sat across from him, sipping a cup of tea. Sitting at the housekeeper's small table and chatting with her felt natural to Shaun, and he again thought of how Maude was like family to him. Actually, even closer than some of his family members.

"You're looking a bit tired. Did the trip go well for you?" Maude took another sip of tea and eyed him with concern.

He swallowed another bite of ham. "It went well, thank you for asking." But as he continued, he shook his head. "But I've got a lot of work ahead of me yet. And I have to make sure I complete this hotel project successfully." He clamped his lips shut before he blathered on to the housekeeper about his innermost feelings.

Maude was not only kind, but had always been a good listener. But Shaun didn't want to concern her with his private turmoil of striving to please his father. Maude had enough work to do in the O'Leary household tolerating Colleen's moods and criticism, so the woman didn't need to be concerned about Shaun's relationship with his father.

"Are you certain you don't want a slice of pie? It's apple, with extra cinnamon on top." Maude winked at him, picked up her tea cup and took it to the sink.

Shaun leaned back in the chair and patted his middle. "As much as I love your pie, I must refuse. That ham and potato salad—not to mention your yeast rolls—have filled me to the brim. But I'm afraid eating so much has only made me sleepy, so I'd better head upstairs."

As he reached the doorway leading from the kitchen into the hallway, Shaun paused and turned around. "Maude, thank you again. Not just for heating up food for me at such a late hour, but for everything." He smiled at her and felt an understanding pass between them.

The woman offered a knowing smile. "It's my pleasure."

Maude knew how much he appreciated all her hard work, and he also understood it wasn't easy putting up with his mother. How would the O'Leary family ever get along without Maude? She certainly was a blessing to them. Hopefully she would remain in their employ for many years to come.

Climbing the oak stairs to the second floor, Shaun realized how weary he was. If only he would sleep well and not lie awake fretting over the work yet to be done in Riverview.

At the thought of Riverview, the image of Sadie formed in his mind, and he couldn't suppress a smile.

"What are you smiling about, brother dear?" Maggie had just stepped out of her room and eyed him.

Shaun forced a casual tone in his reply. "I've only arrived home a little while ago, and Maude heated up some supper for me. Quite delicious, so if I was smiling, I'm sure it was from enjoying her cooking so much." Uncertain as to whether his younger sister would accept his response, he added, "And why are you out of bed? Are you ill?"

Maggie giggled and pulled her robe tighter around her slender form. "No, I'm only going to fetch a cup of water because I'm thirsty. Would you care for some?"

Shaun thanked her and declined, then bade her goodnight. Relieved she hadn't questioned him any more about smiling, he stepped into his room and closed the door behind him.

One thing was certain, Shaun mused as he prepared for bed. If he ever brought Sadie Perkins to the O'Leary home, she'd be welcomed by Maude and Maggie. Perhaps not so much by Shaun's parents, but at least the housekeeper and his sister would be kind and friendly. With those thoughts Shaun climbed into bed and drifted into a heavy slumber only minutes later.

~ ~ ~ ~

"So tell me what Pastor Lucas advised you to do." Lucy leaned forward on the wicker seat, her eyes wide with curiosity. The two women sat on Sadie's front porch, a warm breeze blowing in from the river.

Sadie released a sigh. "He was encouraging, but also realistic. I could tell he wants me to know what I'm getting myself into. Which is good, because I don't want anyone to paint a rosy picture, so to speak. I need to know what to expect if and when I sail to Africa." She hesitated only a moment and clasped her hands underneath her chin. "Sometimes I get so excited at the thought of working with little children in a foreign country and teaching them about Jesus." Sadie's pulse raced.

Lucy reached over to pat her friend's arm. "If you do become a missionary in Africa, you'll be wonderful with those poor little orphans. What a noble venture for you to take on. I admire you so much." A long sigh followed Lucy's words, then her eyes looked down. "But I'll miss you terribly if you go."

Sadie couldn't help thinking that Lucy had missed her calling as an actress on stage. With her dramatic gestures and quick changes in her facial expressions, she would've been a natural, Sadie felt certain. Yet she'd never say those thoughts aloud to her friend. Even though Lucy was full of spirit and could be outspoken, she was also sensitive, and Sadie wouldn't offend her for the world.

Standing and stretching her back, Sadie reassured her friend. "Don't worry. Even if things work out for me to travel to Africa, it won't be forever. I'll return and live in Riverview for the rest of my life." *The rest of my lonely life as an unmarried woman.*

A while later Lucy left, and Sadie returned to her chores. As she scrubbed two of her father's shirts, a nagging thought surfaced in her mind. If she went to Africa—even for a matter of months—who would take care of Papa? Sure, he was capable of doing some tasks around the house, but after working at the lumber mill the man didn't need extra work. Even though some of their neighbors and friends from church would bring meals to Horace, what about his laundry? Would he have to scrub all of his clothing each week, in addition to sweeping and mopping? Would he remember to feed Sadie's beloved cats each day?

The worrisome thoughts tumbled through Sadie's head, making her tired and drained. She paused in her scrubbing and released a long breath. *Pray. Trust.* The two words whispered to her, and she felt a stab of guilt.

Yes, her worries about things that might never come to pass were the result of Sadie not praying enough, and not trusting. She tucked some wayward strands of hair behind her ear and resumed the scrubbing. *Oh Lord, please forgive me for not trusting You as I should. If everything does work out for me to be a missionary, I know You will look after Papa and he will be taken care of. Please forgive my doubts.*

Feeling better after the brief prayer, Sadie completed the laundry and her other chores that afternoon. She prepared the evening meal before Papa arrived home, a little lighter in her spirit. No matter what the future held, the Lord was in control.

While Sadie chopped potatoes, an image of the house on Willow Lane appeared in her mind. Her dream house, that was supposed to be filled with children and lots of laughter.

But if the house was to be demolished and a hotel constructed on that property, how would her dream ever come true? Even if Sadie was called to the mission field, then able to return to Riverview and start her own small orphanage, it wouldn't be in that lovely house. And that bothered Sadie more than she'd ever admit to anyone. Even Lucy.

~ ~ ~ ~

George O'Leary studied the papers spread out on his mahogany desk, adjusting his glasses. "Hmm...yes, looks good. Very good." He glanced at Shaun, standing on the opposite side of the desk.

Shaun had been nervous before showing his father the architect's plans. He'd imagined all sorts of scenarios in his mind early that morning. What if his father wasn't pleased with any of the plans?

Thankfully, it appeared his father was pleased, so Shaun released a huge sigh of relief—at least in his mind. If only the entire hotel project would go so well. Shaun would be considered a success in his father's eyes then.

Trying not to show his obvious relief at his father's reaction, Shaun maintained a casual stance. Keeping his voice level, he shared his upcoming plans for the hotel, and was again relieved at George's positive reaction.

"Since you're handling the hotel, I will have more time to focus on our company's other business projects. I've been thinking about developing a piece of land in Darien, but I'm going to discuss it with Bennett first." George O'Leary offered a dismissive smile to his son, then turned his attention to a stack of papers on one side of his desk.

Shaun returned to his own desk, feeling his stomach tighten after the mention of Mr. Bennett's name. Not that he had anything against the man, but it often bothered Shaun that his father placed so much value on what Joseph Bennett thought.

But why shouldn't George O'Leary place value on his employee's opinions? After all, Joseph Bennett was almost George's age, and had experience in the developing and construction business. Truth be told, Shaun could learn some things from Mr. Bennett. Not to mention the fact that the man had always been polite and friendly to Shaun. But the more involved Shaun became in his father's company, the more he wanted to have a major role, rather than Bennett.

Mentally chiding himself, Shaun decided to stop thinking about the older employee and instead concentrate on what he needed to do. His next steps in making the Riverview hotel a reality were important, so he had to follow through. Which meant, of course, that he needed to return to the town in the near future.

That thought almost made him smile, because when he was in Riverview, that meant more opportunities to see a certain library worker. And the image of her made his heart lighter.

~ ~ ~ ~

"Hello Pastor Lucas. Are you looking for a particular book today?" Polly White greeted the preacher as soon as he'd entered the library.

The medium-built man removed his hat and smiled at the librarian. "No, ma'am. I'm actually here to see Sadie, if she's working today. I was thinking this would be one of her regular days here, and I promise I won't take but a few minutes of her time." He cast a quick glance around the large room, where only a few patrons were milling around and perusing the shelves of books.

"I'm right here, Pastor Lucas." Sadie's voice was followed by her head popping up from behind one of the shelves. With a giggle, she scurried over to greet him. "I was shelving some books on a lower shelf, so that's why you couldn't see me." She smoothed the front of her skirt, then smiled at the preacher.

"I'm sorry to interrupt your work, and I promised Mrs. White I wouldn't take up much of your time. But I wanted to bring over some information I've received." He paused and looked a bit sheepish before continuing. "I suppose I should've waited and stopped by your home this evening, but I felt certain you'd be eager to know about this." He showed her a paper containing names and dollar amounts.

Although the librarian had stepped away from them, Sadie was aware of Polly's curious glances in their direction. As serious as she was, Polly White enjoyed knowing what was going on as much as Dolly Hatcher did, Sadie had noted with amusement more than once.

"What is this?" Sadie had a good idea, but didn't want to seem presumptuous, so she waited for the pastor to explain.

"Remember when we talked recently, and I told you I felt certain some members of our church would be willing to offer some financial support for your mission work? Well, I took the liberty of approaching a few folks, and they were all agreeable to helping you as much as they can. Not only with their financial gifts, but their prayers as well."

Hearing the pastor make those statements made her plans real. She was going to be a missionary. Which was exciting, but also scary. Emotion threatened to overtake her as tears formed in her eyes. Sadie blinked, hoping the pastor didn't notice.

"Oh my, Pastor Lucas. I'm overwhelmed by this kindness." Sadie paused to collect her thoughts. "I-I hardly know what to say, except thank you. I appreciate that you took the time to approach people on my behalf, and appreciate these wonderful folks willing to offer money to help with my mission work." She brought a hand up to her face and swiped at her eyes. Why hadn't she kept a handkerchief in her skirt pocket?

Pastor Lucas reached out and patted her shoulder in a fatherly manner, still smiling at her. "I had a feeling you'd be pleased—and somewhat relieved—to know you've got this support. And I don't want to speak for anyone else, but I honestly feel that when some others in our congregation learn of your plans to work with orphans in Africa, they will also want to contribute." He folded the paper over and handed it to Sadie. "This is your copy to keep. I've also written this information on another paper that I'll keep in my church office." He looked over at Mrs. White and thanked her for allowing him to speak with Sadie, then turned to leave. As he reached the library door, Pastor Lucas paused and turned. "Remember to continue praying about this. And know that others are also praying." He headed out the door.

For a few moments Sadie stood as if frozen to the floor, clutching the paper in both her hands. Drawing in a shaky breath, she knew she'd better explain to the librarian what was going on, as Polly White was about to burst with curiosity.

Hurrying over to the counter where the older woman was stacking some books to be shelved, Sadie hoped there were no traces of the tears that had formed a few minutes earlier. She tucked the paper into the pocket of her skirt, knowing that the names and financial amounts were confidential.

"Thank you for letting me take time to speak with the pastor. You remember I've told you that I've been praying about doing mission work? Pastor Lucas is already getting financial support for my trip to Africa." Sadie smiled, eager to hear her boss's response.

Polly turned to face her, a look of surprise evident on her face. Then she grinned. "Yes, I knew you'd been considering mission work. So this means you're really planning on being a missionary? In Africa?" Her tone held a hint of disbelief.

Sadie nodded. "Yes ma'am. At first I wasn't sure where the Lord would send me, but the more I've prayed and searched my Bible, I feel that's where He wants me to go.

But please don't worry. I plan on giving you enough notice to locate another worker to take my place."

The librarian smiled at Sadie and patted her arm. "I trust you. I am certain you wouldn't just not show up at work one day. And I'm happy for you, if this is what you feel that the Lord has called you to do. I've always admired and respected missionaries, but that is not a job for just anyone." She hesitated before lifting a small stack of books off the counter. "But I'm sure you'll do a wonderful job. And know that I'll also be praying for you." Polly turned and strode toward a shelf.

Several patrons entered the library, so Sadie turned her attention to inquiring if they needed help. To her relief, the remainder of the day passed with no more mention of her mission work plans.

Later that day as she pedaled her bicycle home from the library, Sadie replayed her conversations with the pastor and the librarian. Becoming a missionary was now more of a reality, and that meant she had a lot to do. Even though Sadie had no idea when she'd be sailing to Africa, she needed to prepare for the trip.

Her thoughts were interrupted as a voice called to her. A somewhat familiar male voice. Sadie recognized the voice, then all thoughts of mission work vanished.

~ ~ ~ ~

Not wanting to frighten Sadie and cause her to fall, Shaun didn't call out again, but trotted toward her in silence. Yet she'd heard him, because she was bringing her bicycle to a halt.

When he reached her, he was certain he was grinning like a fool. His thoughts were spinning. He had no idea what to say.

Straddling her bicycle, Sadie smiled shyly at him as she held the handlebars with one hand and smoothed her skirt with the other hand.

"Hello. I didn't expect to see you this afternoon. I was on my way home from my library job." Her eyes held a questioning look, most likely wondering why he'd stopped her.

"I hope I didn't startle you, and I'm sorry if I did. I'm in Riverview for a few days working on a business project and was heading back to the boardinghouse. I'd just finished a meeting at the bank and happened to see you riding past. Again, my apologies if I startled you." He was rambling. What was wrong with him?

Appearing amused, Sadie shook her head. "No apology needed, because you didn't startle me. I hope your meeting went well." She brushed at her skirt again, as though wanting to appear ladylike while straddling her bicycle.

"While I'm in town, would you like to join me for lunch? Perhaps tomorrow if you're not working at the library. I noticed the Gingham Goose Café near the general store, if that suits you."

A slight blush tinted Sadie's cheeks, causing her face to appear even prettier to Shaun.

"That would be nice, if you have time. And no, I'm not working at the library tomorrow, since it's a Thursday. I only work three days a week—Monday, Wednesday, and Friday. The Gingham Goose would be nice."

Before Shaun could offer to hire a carriage and pick up Sadie at her home, she spoke again. "I have some shopping to do tomorrow, so I could ride my bicycle and meet you at the café."

"That sounds good to me. Is twelve o'clock agreeable to you?"

She nodded and offered him that sweet smile, making his insides quiver.

"Thank you. I'll see you then." With those words, Sadie placed her feet on the pedals and continued on her way.

He must look ridiculous standing by the road, staring

after her, so he continued his walk to Miss Callie's boardinghouse. He had a lightness in his steps—and his heart. Even if a real relationship didn't develop between him and Sadie Perkins, he could at least hope. And look forward to spending a brief amount of time with her tomorrow.

"You must've had a productive day. You look happy." Miss Callie was dusting the parlor as Shaun entered the front door of the house. The aroma of savory stew filled the air.

His feelings were obvious. "Yes, ma'am. It was a good day, thank you. I hope you've had a nice day as well. Supper smells delicious, I must add."

Obviously pleased with the compliment, Miss Callie beamed. "The meal should be on the table in forty-five minutes. And yes, thank you. I've had a good day myself."

After the evening meal, Shaun attempted to read, but couldn't focus. All he could think of was his lunch date with Sadie the next day. He hoped to learn more about her, but didn't want to pepper her with questions.

Hopefully Sadie wouldn't ask many questions about his family. If she realized how wealthy the O'Leary family was, it might discourage a relationship from developing. Although he barely knew her, Shaun had a feeling that Sadie Perkins was an unpretentious, hard-working woman—so opposite the Savannah debutantes his mother wanted him to pursue. With that thought, he prepared for bed and smiled to himself. He could only imagine the reaction of his parents if they knew he was interested in a small-town librarian.

Chapter Five

"You seem lighthearted this evening, Sadie-girl. You must've had a very good day at the library." Horace grinned at his daughter. She placed their meal on the kitchen table.

To her dismay, Sadie knew that annoying blush was creeping up her face. Maybe her father wouldn't notice. Or if he did, perhaps he would think her face was pink from being near the hot stove.

"I did have a nice day. How about you? Any big news at the mill?" She set a glass of milk next to her father's plate, then poured herself a cup of tea.

"Only the usual talk about that fancy hotel our town's s'posed to be gettin'. It's downright crazy, but there must be some truth, because the story is still goin' round." Horace shook his head, then waited until Sadie was seated to offer up their blessing. Afterward, Horace continued, with Sadie listening intently.

"Yep, the fellars are sayin' that piece of land on Willow Lane is where the hotel will be. But it's such a shame to tear down that nice house." He made a tsk sound, then began eating his sliced beef and potatoes.

Sadie's earlier happy mood plummeted, but she fought it. "Yes, Lucy told me about that, and I think it's terrible. That's the house Mama and I always enjoyed looking at when I was a little girl. On our walks we always stopped in front of that house." Her mood continued to sink, and her father appeared pensive at hearing her words.

"I'd forgotten you and your mother took those walks together. Now I remember." He had a far-away look in his tired eyes, most likely thinking of his late wife.

Determined to lighten the conversation, Sadie shared an amusing incident that had happened at the library that day. When she told her father about a child trying to balance a book on his head and Polly White's reaction, Sadie giggled. With relief, she saw her father chuckling too.

"I can imagine Mrs. White wasn't fond of one of her library books being used in that manner." Horace shook his head, still chuckling.

"No, she wasn't. And that poor child had a look of fear on his face when the book tumbled from his head and landed with a loud noise on the library floor. Then his mother bent over to pick up the book, but the poor woman dropped the books she was holding. I suppose that's the most excitement the library has had in a while." Sadie laughed.

Cleaning the kitchen a little while later, her thoughts returned to Shaun O'Leary and their lunch date the next day. She'd decided it best not to mention anything to her father—at least not yet. After all, this might be the only time Sadie met the man for a meal. She'd need to be careful and guard her feelings.

But deep inside, she hoped this would be the first of many times she would enjoy the company of the handsome man from Savannah. Hopefully he'd continue being as nice as he'd been so far, because Sadie not only found him attractive, but charming and kind too. Almost too good to be true. She pushed that thought from her mind. She'd already been jilted by a beau and did not intend for that to happen again.

~ ~ ~ ~

To Sadie's relief, the next day dawned sunny and pleasant—a perfect day to ride her bicycle. When she'd gone to bed the night before she had fretted that if it rained the next day, she'd be a dripping mess when she arrived at the café. Thankfully that wasn't a concern.

Pedaling to the Gingham Goose Café, her stomach began doing flips. Although she enjoyed the food there, today she most likely wouldn't be able to eat much.

Another thought didn't help her stomach calm down, and she gripped her handlebars as she pedaled underneath the tall oaks. Had she seemed too eager to meet Shaun for lunch? When he'd asked her, she hadn't hesitated, but replied right away about meeting him for lunch. Oh, how she hoped her reply didn't sound as though she was desperate to have a date with a man.

Approaching the café, Sadie offered up a hasty prayer for guidance. There was no denying she was attracted to Shaun, and he must find her at least a little appealing. But with her plans to do mission work in the not-too-distant future, Sadie didn't need to consider a serious relationship with any man, not even one as handsome and charming as Shaun O'Leary.

As though her thoughts made him appear, the man stepped out of the café the moment she pedaled onto the sidewalk. She guided her bicycle closer to the building, then climbed off and set the kickstand. Smoothing her dress, Sadie knew eyes watched her. Shaun O'Leary's eyes.

"Right on time. I've already secured a table for us, as I was afraid the café would fill up quickly since it's lunchtime." He took her arm and guided her to a table next to a side wall, away from most of the other tables.

"Thank you. This is a treat. I dine here now and then, but not very often. The food is always delicious." She placed her reticule on the floor between her chair and the wall, so it wouldn't be stepped upon.

After ordering their food, Shaun kept the conversation flowing. He discussed the differences of a small town such as Riverview and the larger port city of Savannah. Then he asked her about the library, and details about her job.

When their food arrived, the server placed the steaming vegetables in front of them. Sadie's stomach rumbled. Perhaps she would be able to eat, after all.

Noticing that Shaun did not offer to say a blessing, Sadie bowed her head briefly and offered up a silent prayer of thanks for the meal.

"This is delicious." He smiled before taking another bite of his mashed potatoes.

Sadie was relieved he was pleased with his meal. So far there had been no moments of awkward silence. She enjoyed a few more bites of her beans and corn, then wiped her mouth with the crisp linen napkin.

"Please tell me about your work. You live in Savannah, but you mentioned you're working on a project here in Riverview. Is that correct?" Sadie sipped her lemonade, awaiting his response.

With a nod, Shaun eyed her in a curious manner, as though hesitant to speak. Releasing a sigh, he leaned in over the table. Sadie couldn't imagine what he was about to say. Surely he wasn't involved in any unsavory activity?

"I work for my father's company, based in Savannah where we live. We are a land development company, and oversee construction projects." He paused, looking directly into Sadie's eyes.

Not certain how to respond, Sadie nodded, hoping he'd offer more information.

He cleared his throat. "Presently, we are preparing to build a hotel here in Riverview. Perhaps you've heard about it? I'm sure in small towns the news travels fast." He chuckled and gazed across the table at her.

Suppressing a gasp, Sadie's eyes widened. "You are the man behind the hotel I've heard about?" She hoped her question didn't sound rude, but she was stunned. How could she not have already figured out that Shaun O'Leary was in Riverview to oversee the hotel? It all added up now.

Appearing embarrassed, Shaun nodded. "Um...yes, that would be me. Is it bad that I'm working on that project? Our hope is that having a high-quality hotel here in your small town will benefit Riverview's economy."

Dazed at learning this news, Sadie tried to force a smile on her face, but it wouldn't come. She shrugged and moistened her lips, hoping her voice wouldn't come out in a squeak. "I-I'm just surprised that you're the one working on the hotel. I had no idea. To be honest, I didn't know who was responsible for the construction of the hotel." She clamped her lips together. No need to say words she'd regret. Finding out more information was what Sadie needed to do. Perhaps the hotel was not going to be built where her dream house sat, but she was almost afraid to ask.

Shaun spoke matter-of-factly, with his hands clasped together on the table. "We still have a long way to go on this project, but I'm waiting for the final approval on the purchase of the land. I've already hired an architect to draw up plans for the hotel, but there's much to be done yet. That's why I'm renting a room at Miss Callie's boarding house." He smiled as though he'd shared something amusing.

But there was nothing amusing about a hotel being built where a beautiful house already stood. Sadie drew in a breath and asked about the location.

"Willow Lane. There's a nice piece of land that should be ideal for the kind of hotel my father and I have in mind. Not too large, but just right for a town the size of Riverview."

Sadie's head was swimming. She grabbed her glass of lemonade and took a sip. Unfortunately the liquid went down wrong and she choked. Grabbing her linen napkin to cover her mouth, Sadie tried to control her coughs. A helpless feeling washed over her.

Shaun jumped up from his chair and rushed over to her, leaning in only inches from her face. "Are you okay? Do you need some water? That might be better than drinking lemonade." Concern filled his face as he touched her shoulder.

By that time their server, a young woman a little younger than Sadie, appeared and inquired if they needed help.

The coughing subsided and Sadie looked up. "I'm fine." The words came out in a whisper, and she sent an embarrassed smile to both their server and to Shaun. The last thing she wanted to do was cause a scene in the restaurant.

After returning to his seat, Shaun gave her a look of compassion. "I'm so sorry you were choked. I know that's a scary feeling. For a few seconds I was afraid you were about to be sick." He reached across the table and patted her hand. "Are you certain you wouldn't rather drink some water?"

Sadie hated the tingle that coursed through her when he touched her hand. She assured him the lemonade was fine and the coughing spell had passed. "I didn't mean to make a scene. I guess the lemonade went down the wrong way." But she knew the information she'd learned about the hotel's location hadn't helped.

At that moment, Pastor and Mrs. Lucas paused at their table, on their way to a table in the back corner. Sadie introduced Shaun, and he and the pastor exchanged pleasantries. Sadie couldn't help noticing Mrs. Lucas grinning at her.

After the pastor and his wife went on to their table, Shaun asked if Sadie would like dessert.

"Oh, goodness no. I'm much too full, but thank you. My

meal was delicious, but I'd better go on my errands now. I'm sure you have work to do." She was relieved the conversation hadn't returned to the hotel. Sadie did not want to think about that right now.

"Thank you for having lunch with me, and I do hope to see you again soon." Shaun's eyes lingered on her face.

With a parting smile, she hurried to her bicycle parked on the sidewalk. Shaun was inside the café paying for their lunch, and she was eager to climb onto her bicycle and pedal to the store. She wouldn't allow herself to think about anything except what she needed at Hatcher's Store. Her dream house being torn down was now a reality, and that thought sent waves of sadness through her.

~ ~ ~ ~

Why had Sadie looked so strange when he'd mentioned building the hotel on Willow Lane? Shaun couldn't shake the puzzled feeling, and he regretted not discussing it more at lunch with her. But after her pastor and his wife had stopped at their table and chatted, there wasn't any time left. He had an appointment to keep at the bank, after all.

Now slowing his steps as he prepared to enter the brick building on Riverview's main street, Shaun tried to force thoughts of Sadie from his mind. He must focus on business, and what he was in town to accomplish. If his father was going to be proud of him, Shaun had to make it happen. And that required focus and hard work.

"Good afternoon, Mr. O'Leary." The bank president greeted him.

Shaun's footsteps echoed on the freshly-waxed floor. There were only two other bank customers at the moment, so the lobby was quiet. An unexpected twinge of nervousness skittered through him but he tried to ignore the feeling. Pasting a smile on his face, Shaun returned the greeting and extended his hand.

Mr. Withers led Shaun into the same small conference room where they'd met the previous times. "You'll be relieved to know everything is now finalized. By signing this last document, the property on Willow Lane officially belongs to O'Leary Land Development Company." Mr. Withers appeared satisfied with this information, and even more pleased when Shaun reacted in a positive manner.

Thirty minutes later, Shaun exited the bank building, feeling as though a weight had been lifted from his shoulders. He had panicked after receiving a telegram from the banker stating that another document had been located. Now he breathed a huge sigh of relief and was eager to get the construction underway.

Of course, there was still the matter of tearing down the house that stood on the land. Why did that bother him so much? Shaun had no ties to the house, nor did he know any of the past occupants. Yes, it was a lovely house, but there were many other lovely houses in towns throughout the south. In his own hometown of Savannah there were beautiful mansions, including the O'Leary home. It wasn't as though a stately home was a rarity.

Without giving any thought to what he was doing, Shaun headed the three blocks toward Willow Lane. He took in the sights of the sleepy little town. and suppressed a grin while imagining the difference an upscale hotel would make in Riverview. Not only creating jobs, but in a sense the hotel could make the town a better-known place. The location on the banks of the Altamaha River was an added benefit for the town, and Shaun was surprised no one prior to his father had attempted to build a hotel there. Or, perhaps someone had tried, but lacked the financial backing to follow through.

Reaching Willow Lane, Shaun was greeted by birdsong. It was almost as though the trees along either side of the street were filled with the feathered creatures, ready to present a concert for Shaun. The Live oaks stood regal and proud, many of them draped with Spanish moss. The few houses located on the street—with the exception of the one his father was purchasing to be demolished—all appeared to have residents. The houses were well-cared for, with neat yards and trimmed shrubs. Clusters of flowers bloomed here and there in the yards, the touch of color adding even more appeal to the area.

How would the families living on this street feel about having a hotel in their midst? Would they view it as something positive for the community, and even exciting? Or would they be resentful, feeling the hotel didn't belong in their area?

Reaching the plot of land, he stood on the sidewalk viewing the house and the trees around it. Try as he might, for some strange reason he could not imagine the hotel standing on that property. He'd been able to visualize it before, especially after meeting with the architect. But at that moment, all Shaun saw was a beautiful house surrounded by trees and foliage. A house that would make a wonderful home for a family.

~ ~ ~ ~

On Saturday a knock sounded at Sadie's front door, and she hurried to answer, thinking it might be Lucy. To her surprise, it was Pastor Lucas, appearing rather embarrassed.

"Hello Sadie. I apologize for dropping by when you're not expecting me, but I felt the need to explain something."

After inviting him in, Sadie offered the pastor a cup of lemonade, although she was bursting with curiosity as to the nature of his visit.

He declined, then explained his reason for being there. "When I saw you and the gentleman at the Gingham Goose Café a few days ago, I refrained from making mention of your mission work, and did not want you to think I'd forgotten about your plans. I was unsure if you'd shared your desire to do mission work with others—specifically the gentleman you were with that day." The pastor paused, a sheepish look on his face.

Sadie was touched at his concern. "I never thought you'd forgotten about my plans, or the talk we had recently concerning my mission work. I appreciate that you didn't mention it in front of Mr. O'Leary, although it would've been fine." At the mention of Shaun's name, Sadie's face warmed. Hopefully her pastor didn't notice.

Immense relief covered the man's face and he beamed. "Very good. Now, the other reason I've stopped by today is to let you know what I've found out regarding your mission work. Two more members of our congregation have offered to help with the financial arrangements, and I've taken the liberty of inquiring about your voyage to Africa."

Listening to the pastor share more details, Sadie was dazed. Was this a dream? Was she actually making plans to sail across the ocean to a foreign land?

Ten minutes later, Sadie bade him good-bye, closed the door behind him, and tears stung her eyes. It was all so much. Her emotions rode on a whirlwind with a mixture of excitement, fear, and nervousness.

Before returning to her chores, she needed a cup of tea. After putting the kettle on to boil, Sadie took her Bible from the shelf in the living room, then returned to the kitchen table. As she sat a few minutes later sipping the tea and reading verses from her Bible, a sense of peace washed over her. She knew that no matter what lay ahead, the Lord was with her, guiding and leading her.

If she would only remember that and not let her emotions take control, she'd be fine.

Without any bidding, the image of Shaun O'Leary appeared in her mind, and she drew in a deep breath. Not that it mattered, but Sadie was curious as to what he would say about her plans to serve as a missionary.

Regardless of his or anyone else's feelings, Sadie would do what she felt called to do, and at the present time, she felt called to serve as a missionary, to work with orphans on another continent. If only that continent wasn't so far across the ocean.

~ ~ ~ ~

"Sadie girl, this is some o' the best stew you've ever made." Horace grinned before scooping up another spoonful.

Giggling, Sadie shook her head. "I think you're just really hungry this evening, so that's why you think the stew tastes so good."

The pair ate in silence for a few moments, then Sadie decided to share details of the pastor's unexpected visit with her father.

To her relief, Papa nodded and smiled as she told him about the financial support she'd already received, thanks to Pastor Lucas.

"The pastor is even gathering information for me about sailing to Africa. He's going to let me know when I need to book my voyage." An unexpected shudder ran through her. She grabbed her cup and took a sip of water.

Horace eyed her curiously. "What is it? Are you feelin' sick all of a sudden?"

Not wanting to alarm her father, Sadie shook her head. "No, I'm fine. Just had a little chill running through me. Maybe I've been eating too fast." She didn't want to be dishonest with her father, but knew if she told him what she was thinking, he'd be more than a little concerned. Likely her father would insist she change her plans.

Yet the thought of sailing across the vast Atlantic Ocean made her nervous, especially given the fact she'd only been on the water when she and Lucy rode the ferry to St. Simon's Island. That ride wouldn't even compare to sailing on the open sea for days. Her stomach tightened. For Papa's sake, Sadie must appear strong and not worried.

Changing the subject, Sadie chattered about her small

garden patch. "It's amazing how quickly those weeds come up again, so soon after I've pulled them all." She shook her head.

"That's just part of gardenin' but you're right. It's a nuisance to keep pullin' those weeds." Her father still eyed her, although the conversation was light. Minutes later, the meal was finished, and Horace complimented her cooking, yet again. After one more glance at her, he ambled into the living room to read the evening newspaper.

While washing the dishes and tidying the kitchen, Sadie tried to keep her thoughts away from her earlier feeling. That shudder coursing through her at dinner had been so strange. Could that mean she would have a difficult time sailing? She chided herself. How else would she be a missionary to Africa if she didn't travel there by a ship?

Trust and pray. The silent reminder seemed to whisper to her again. Her call to serve as a missionary didn't mean everything would fall into place for her. Sadie knew she had much to do in order to be prepared for her journey to Africa. Not only physical preparations, but spiritual preparations as well.

She was thankful tomorrow was Sunday, because being at church would help her gain peace about the situation. Pastor Lucas always preached excellent sermons, so hopefully his words would calm her heart about her mission work.

With uplifted spirits, Sadie finished her chores and curled up with the novel she was reading. As her two cats snuggled next to her, Sadie felt a warmth and contentment. No matter what her future held, the Lord was in control.

~ ~ ~ ~

Miss Callie set the bowl of steaming grits and a platter of bacon on the dining table. The aromas of eggs and biscuits were now joined by the grits and bacon, and Shaun could hardly wait to begin eating.

He'd quickly learned that one of Miss Callie's rules was a blessing must be given before each meal, no matter how hungry her boarders happened to be.

As soon as the amens were said, each man began serving his plate. The talking was limited, which was fine with Shaun, because he wasn't in a mood to visit much that morning. Miss Callie's earlier comment still hovered in his mind, and he couldn't shake it.

When Shaun had entered the dining room that morning, Miss Callie immediately asked him if he planned on attending church while in Riverview. Although she didn't ask the question in a judgmental tone, Shaun bristled right away.

"No ma'am. I don't plan on attending a church while here. But thank you for asking." His reply sounded awkward, and he wondered if she expected him to explain.

Miss Callie had nodded in her no-nonsense manner, then continued setting the table. But a matter of seconds later she surprised him. "The reason I was asking you that question is that I always tell my boarders if they want to hear a good sermon, Pastor Lucas at the Riverview church delivers a mighty fine message each week." With that, she clamped her lips shut as if she'd done her duty and continued on with her work.

Relieved that there was no more talk about church, Shaun enjoyed his hearty breakfast in silence. There was no doubt about it—Miss Callie was a wonderful cook. Of course, Shaun would always be partial to Maude, and the very thought of the O'Leary's housekeeper almost brought a smile to his face. He hoped his family was treating her well in his absence. He'd be happy to see Maude when he returned home the next week.

"Thank you. The breakfast was very tasty." Shaun grinned at the older woman. Two of the other men were still eating and nodded to Shaun before he headed out.

Deciding to take a walk, Shaun left the boarding house and ambled toward the business area of Riverview. The sleepy town appeared even quieter this Sunday morning, but it was peaceful and calming, so Shaun enjoyed himself. If his father's company was investing in a major building project in the town, he should be as familiar as possible with the layout of the area.

Without giving it much thought, he headed toward the river, feeling the early May heat hanging in the air. Shaun knew that come summer, the area would be humid, especially close to a river.

The dock at the small Riverview port had only a couple of boats tied up—a sharp contrast to the bustling Savannah port, with its usual busyness and cargo vessels. Although Shaun was fond of his hometown, he was developing a growing attraction to the much smaller town of Riverview. But was it only the town? The question tugged at him as he approached the river. No, he was attracted to one particular resident of Riverview, and try as he might, Shaun couldn't stop thinking about her.

After strolling along the dock and viewing the river, Shaun headed back toward the streets. Following the sidewalk, he walked along the residential areas and admired some of the houses.

Church bells pealed, sending out a sweet and touching melody. Up ahead on his right stood the Riverview Church, a neat-looking stone building with wooden doors painted red. The few windows along either side were stained glass, and Shaun admired them from afar. He'd enjoy a closer look, but that would mean attending a church service, something he had no intention of doing.

People were trickling into the building, and with a quick glance at his watch, Shaun realized the time was approaching eleven o'clock. The service must be about to begin, and he was relieved Miss Callie wasn't entering the building at that moment. She'd most likely beckon him into the church. How awkward that would be.

A small group of adults approaching the doors caught Shaun's attention. Two older men, an older woman, and a young woman. *Sadie.* Yes, he was certain it was Sadie Perkins entering the church building with several other adults—all a bit older than her.

The breeze gently blew her chestnut mane, and her pink dress fluttered as she walked up the steps into the building. Thankfully she didn't see Shaun, but he had no doubt the woman was Sadie. And he wasn't surprised at all that she attended this church.

Returning to the boarding house a little later, the image of Sadie resurfaced in Shaun's mind. Why did simply catching a glimpse of her make him feel like a young schoolboy? What was it about the woman that pulled at him so?

Shaun wasn't sure, but he was sure he wanted to get closer to her, and learn more about her.

~ ~ ~ ~

"The sermon today was wonderful, wasn't it?" Lucy sipped her lemonade while seated on Sadie's porch. Birds chirped in the nearby trees, and butterflies flitted through the air.

Sadie nodded in agreement. "Pastor Lucas always has an excellent message. And today's theme about trusting the Lord seemed to be meant especially for me." She chuckled but then realized her friend appeared pensive. "What is it?"

Lucy shook her head and shrugged. "Oh, I'm just being a silly daydreamer. But I couldn't help noticing all the married couples in church and I—" Lucy hesitated only a moment, then continued. "I'm only sharing this because you're my very best friend. But I kept thinking how wonderful it would be if I was married again, and my husband was sitting beside me." A giggle burst from Lucy's lips, and she covered her mouth. "Listen to me—carrying on like a young schoolgirl."

Sadie grinned and patted her friend's hand. "I think it's fine to daydream, Lucy. I've done it myself, you know. But I have to ask you—as your best friend, of course—does Matthew figure into this daydream you were having?" She arched an eyebrow, eager to hear her friend's response.

Lucy's face grew crimson. "Yes, but I wouldn't share this with another soul. I know we only met last month, and there's still much I don't know about Matthew. But he seems so kind, not to mention he's a Christian man and he's handsome." Lucy sipped the last bit of her lemonade.

"Yes, I agree. In my opinion he seems like the ideal man for you. So I'm hoping and praying that if he is meant for you, things will work out soon. Because I know that's what you want." Sadie finished her drink and stood from the wicker chair to stretch her legs and back. A breeze ruffled her skirt, although the temperature had grown warmer since they'd been sitting on the porch.

"I'd better return home and help Mother with our evening meal. I'm truly blessed that my dear parents provide a home for me, and I am grateful. But I so look forward to being a wife again and keeping house in my own home." She offered a wistful smile, then gave Sadie a quick hug before turning to leave the porch.

"I understand. I promise I do." She watched her friend leave, then gathered their cups and carried them inside to the kitchen.

Later as Sadie prepared the evening meal for Papa and herself, she reflected on Lucy's words about wanting to be a wife and have her own home. Her thoughts traveled further, and she imagined Lucy and Matthew married, living in Riverview. Then she imagined herself married, living in the lovely house on Willow Lane. *But married to what man?* Her thoughts teased her, but deep in her heart there was only one man whose face formed in her mind. Shaun O'Leary.

But there were still too many unanswered questions about him, besides the fact he lived in Savannah, rather than Riverview. She was reminded that the man Lucy had feelings for didn't live in Riverview either. In fact, Matthew lived on an island, so he couldn't even take a train to visit Lucy.

Why was she thinking about marriage anyway? A chiding voice scolded her as she chopped potatoes and carrots. Her calling was to become a missionary and work with orphans. Then, Lord willing, she'd return to Riverview and start a home for children here. Even if it wasn't in her dream house on Willow Lane. Those were her plans, and a man—Shaun O'Leary or any other man—was not part of her plans.

~ ~ ~ ~

Monday afternoon Shaun headed to the Riverview library, anticipating a visit with Sadie. Since this was one of her days to work, he felt certain she'd be there, but he hoped she wouldn't be too busy.

As he walked along the sidewalk his thoughts reflected on what he'd accomplished that day. Not that much, but at least some progress on the hotel plans. Since Miss Callie had been kind enough to allow him use of the boardinghouse dining room table when it wasn't mealtime, Shaun decided to do his work there during the day.

He'd studied the architect's drawings, made pages of notes, and then later walked over to the property on Willow Lane. It was still difficult to ignore the lovely house standing on the property, but Shaun had to make himself visualize the hotel located there instead.

Entering the library, he spotted Sadie behind the counter. To Shaun's relief there were no patrons at the counter, so he slowly approached her.

As her eyes met his, a smile lit her face, and a tiny bit of pink colored her cheeks. "Hello. Are you here for a book?" Of course, she'd asked that.

Shaun shook his head and grinned. "No, I'm here to see one of the library employees. I believe her name is Sadie." He hoped his teasing didn't make him appear a fool.

She giggled and spread her hands. "At your service." Then she shot a quick glance over toward the left, and he followed her gaze. The librarian was speaking with a patron behind one of the shelves, apparently searching for a book. Shaun supposed Sadie was making certain her boss wasn't observing them. He had no intentions of causing trouble for Sadie at her job.

"I won't stay long, but did want to stop in and say hello. Did you have a nice weekend?" He hoped his tone sounded casual, and not like he was checking up on her.

"Yes, thank you. My father and I always attend the Riverview church on Sundays, and that's always nice. Whenever you're in town on a Sunday, you are welcome to join us." She smiled sweetly up at him, and to his dismay he was at a loss for words.

This did not seem like the appropriate time to explain his feelings toward God, so he merely smiled and thanked her. "Since tomorrow is Tuesday, would you join me for lunch again? That is, if you don't already have plans." He held his breath as he awaited her reply. Oh, how he wanted to spend more time with this lovely woman.

Sadie moistened her lips and appeared to be giving the question some thought. Then she grinned and nodded. "Yes, thank you. That sounds nice. Shall we meet again at the Gingham Goose Café?"

"That's fine, unless you'd prefer that I come to your home to escort you to the café. I don't mind."

"Oh no, I enjoy riding my bicycle, and then I can stop by the general store after I leave the café, as I did last week. That works out perfectly for me."

At that moment Polly White approached the counter and

smiled at Shaun. "Hello there. How nice to see you again. Is Miss Perkins assisting you?" A tiny bit of mischief gleamed in Polly's eyes, which surprised Shaun. Perhaps there was a playful side to the serious librarian.

"Hello, it's nice to see you also. I had a few minutes this afternoon and wanted to stop in and say hello to Miss Perkins. And you too, of course." He hoped his added comment sounded sincere.

Thankfully, the librarian appeared pleased at his friendly manner, and if Shaun wasn't mistaken, the older woman even blushed at his comment.

Deciding he'd better be getting back to the boarding house and clear his papers from the dining room table before the evening meal, Shaun bade Sadie and Polly good-bye, with his eyes lingering on Sadie.

Returning to Miss Callie's, Shaun had the urge to skip along the sidewalk. He almost laughed aloud as he imagined stares he'd receive from passers-by. Yes, he was being silly. Yet, another opportunity to be with the lovely Sadie gave him a burst of happiness. If only he didn't have to return to Savannah, then he could see her each day. *Calm down, O'Leary. You don't know how she feels about you. Better not try to move too fast with a relationship.*

In spite of the chiding voice in his mind, Shaun allowed his thoughts to imagine a real relationship with the beautiful woman. Another burst of happiness coursed through him as he thought of Sadie, happiness he'd not experienced in a long time.

~ ~ ~ ~

What had she done? Only two days ago Sadie had given herself a silent talk about her missionary plans. Now it was Tuesday and she was riding her bicycle to meet Shaun for lunch—again—at the Gingham Goose. *Why am I doing this?* She gripped her handlebars in frustration.

Sadie was so preoccupied with her private thoughts she had to swerve to miss a man walking along the sidewalk. She needed to be more careful when she was riding, regardless of where her mind happened to be.

There was no denying she was attracted to Shaun O'Leary. What young woman wouldn't be? Yet a future with any man was not a part of her plans. Her focus needed to be on her mission work. To add to her conflicting feelings, it seemed the more she was with Shaun the more she wanted to be with him. That was not a good thing. She huffed out an unladylike sigh, knowing she needed to put these thoughts aside for now.

Arriving at the café, Sadie parked her bicycle in the usual spot, then smoothed her skirt and clutched her reticule. Before she could open the door, it swung toward her, causing her to jump. Shaun stood in the café doorway, grinning and looking more handsome than ever. No, this wasn't good.

"Hello. I hope you're hungry, because the server has informed me the chef is cooking a delicious stew today." He gestured her into the café, which was filled with a delectable aroma.

She smiled, sitting in the chair he'd pulled out for her, while willing herself to act calm. What was wrong with her? She shouldn't feel so nervous. But deep inside her heart, Sadie knew the reason.

"You seem quiet today. Are you feeling well? Perhaps you'd like some tea rather than water." His dark eyes held concern. His gaze seemed to be searching the depths of her thoughts.

She drew in a breath, then shook her head. "I'm fine, and no thank you. This water is good." She took a quick sip to emphasize her response.

After setting her glass on the table, Sadie dabbed her lips and looked at Shaun. "How is your work here in Riverview?" She attempted to keep her voice level and devoid of any emotion.

A curious look appeared on his face, but only for a matter of seconds, and then it was gone. He smiled. "Very well, thank you for asking. This hotel will be the first major project that my father has assigned to me, and I'll admit I was a bit anxious in the beginning. But with each step accomplished, I breathe a sigh of relief." He chuckled.

Sadie forced a polite smile, but didn't comment. Thankfully her hands were in her lap since her fists were now clenched.

"Now this next step might prove to be a hurdle. Before construction can begin, the house presently occupying the land must be torn down. It is a shame, because it appears to be a lovely house, although it needs some work. I was surprised no one lives there, to be honest. But since no one does, and my father's company is able to purchase the property, then we'll have no choice but to have the structure demolished." Shaun shrugged, then greeted their server who set bowls of hot stew, a small plate of yeast rolls, and a saucer of butter on the table.

Sadie had no appetite, and even worse, her pulse raced with anger. She must control her emotions and not make a scene. Not that she'd ever made a scene in her life. Her hands were now fisted so tightly she feared her fingernails would dig into her flesh.

As soon as the server departed, Sadie bowed her head and whispered a hasty blessing for the food, adding a silent prayerful plea she'd not say anything she would regret. Then she forced herself to relax her hands and make attempts at eating.

Shaun held his spoon, waiting for Sadie to begin eating. But she couldn't. Try as she might, Sadie could not take a bite of her stew at that moment.

"Is something wrong? Would you prefer to order something different? It's no problem if you would rather eat something else." Concern was again evident on his face, only adding to the jumble of emotions coursing through her.

She shook her head. "No, thank you. The stew will be delicious, I'm sure. I don't want to burn my tongue, so I'll let mine cool a bit."

"Okay, but if you decide you'd prefer something else, I'll be happy to order whatever you want." His smile held warmth and charm, and normally Sadie would've been flattered and pleased.

Yet at the moment she had the strong urge to inform Shaun that what she wanted was the house on Willow Lane. Or at least for the house to remain standing, rather than being torn down for a hotel to be constructed in its place. Riverview didn't even need a big, fancy hotel anyway. Their town was not a resort area, and the residents of Riverview—at the least the ones Sadie knew—did not care a whit about attracting tourists to their town.

The thoughts rushing in her mind yearned to be spoken aloud to the man seated across from her, yet Sadie would regret the words later. So she sat in silence, waiting for her stomach and nerves to calm and her stew to cool. By now her head was beginning to throb, so she took another sip of water, avoiding Shaun's curious gaze.

Despite his concern, Shaun apparently had no idea of the effect his statements had caused. After he swallowed a bite of yeast roll, he grinned at her. "Well, enough talk about my job. I want to hear about you. You've mentioned that you enjoy reading to the children in the library, and I'm sure they adore you. Do you have any nieces or nephews?" He buttered another roll.

"No, I'm an only child, so no nieces or nephews. But yes, I do enjoy my time with the children who come into the library. That's my favorite part of my job." She slowly took a bite of her stew. Perhaps eating would help calm her tension and ease her headache.

"Would you like to have children of your own someday?" Shaun's question came out casually, as if he'd commented on the weather.

To her dismay, Sadie choked and grabbed her glass of water. Trying not to cause a scene with her coughs, she took tiny sips of the cold liquid and drew in slow breaths. Thankfully the coughing spell didn't last long. What she noticed was Shaun's reaction—obviously prepared to leap from his chair if necessary. He'd scooted back a bit and had moved his linen napkin from his lap to the table. He watched her intently with worry-filled eyes.

"Are you okay now? Did you choke on your stew?" His questions came out softly, as though not wanting to embarrass her. There was a hint of tenderness in his questions.

Sadie thanked him. "I'm fine. I must've swallowed my stew too quickly." There was no way she would reveal the true reason for her choking episode. His unexpected question about having children had almost taken the wind out of her. Especially coming from the attractive man across from her.

At that moment a man stopped at their table, speaking to Shaun. He was one of the boarders at Miss Callie's, and he and Shaun visited for a few minutes before he exited the café.

After the man left, the conversation didn't return to the topic of children, to Sadie's relief. Instead, she questioned Shaun about Savannah, and the differences in the larger city and a small town such as Riverview.

He seemed more than happy to share details about his home city, and the remainder of their lunch passed quickly. As the couple left the café, Sadie thanked Shaun for the stew, apologizing for choking and coughing.

"No apology needed. You couldn't help that coughing spell, and I'm glad you're okay." He paused, then looked into her eyes as if wanting to say something important. But he only commented about his schedule. "I have to return to Savannah in the next day or so, but I'll be back in Riverview next week, for certain. I'd like to see you again, if that's agreeable with you." He looked hopeful and reached out and clasped her hand.

Tingles rushed through her, and all she could do was smile. After climbing onto her bicycle, she looked back at Shaun, who was walking in the opposite direction toward the boardinghouse.

"Thank you again for my lunch. I'll see you again next week." As Sadie spoke, Shaun turned and waved. Was it her imagination, or did his face light up at her last comment?

~ ~ ~ ~

Something had upset her at lunch, Shaun was certain. As he returned to his work on the hotel plans that afternoon, he couldn't stop thinking about Sadie. Her entire mood had changed after he'd mentioned the house on Willow Lane. Specifically, tearing down the house on Willow Lane. Did Sadie have some sort of connection to that house? Shaun couldn't help wondering. Sadie had never mentioned having relatives who'd resided there, but perhaps she was private about her family. After all, he was still getting to know her. But it was all puzzling to him.

At least she was agreeable to seeing him again. When he returned from Savannah, he planned on contacting her as soon as possible. At the moment, he'd better focus on the hotel plans, and then get his bags ready to catch a train the next morning.

Promptly at six o'clock, Miss Callie served the boarders a delicious meal of fried chicken, potatoes, and green beans. Her biscuits were feather-light, and Shaun helped himself to a second one, spreading a lavish amount of butter on it. The conversation was sparse, as the men were too busy eating.

As they were finishing the meal, the man who'd seen Shaun in the café that day spoke up. "That was a lovely lady with you today, Mr. O'Leary."

Shaun smiled. He didn't want to discuss Sadie with

anyone, lest rumors start in this small town. Too late, because Miss Callie overheard as she refilled glasses with water.

With an arched eyebrow, she teased Shaun. "So, you've met one of Riverview's charming ladies already, Mr. O'Leary?" She poured more water into his glass.

Hoping he didn't sound defensive, Shaun shrugged. "She's a friend, and yes, she is lovely." Before anyone else could comment, Shaun pushed away from the table and thanked Callie for the meal. "I am stuffed, Miss Callie. Thank you so much. And just a reminder that I'll be heading out after breakfast tomorrow to return to Savannah. I should be returning to Riverview within the week." He downed the remainder of his water, relieved no one else commented on Sadie.

Try as he might, Shaun could not stop thinking about the change in Sadie's mood earlier that day. But his concentration needed to be on the hotel and all the work that still lay ahead of him. He would see Sadie again when he returned to Riverview and try to discover her connection with the Willow Lane house. If there was even a connection. Perhaps something else had been bothering her at lunch. But what could it be? Things had seemed pleasant until Shaun mentioned his work.

The next morning he ate his breakfast as quickly as possible, hoping to avoid any questions about Sadie from the other boarders. Thankfully the two men who joined him at the table downed their food without any conversation. The only sounds were the clinking of silverware scraping the plates.

An hour later Shaun was on the train headed to Savannah. He forced thoughts of Sadie from his mind, and instead planned what must be accomplished next. But feelings of uneasiness accompanied that thought. The next step would be lining up the demolition crew to tear down the house on the property, in addition to clearing away some of the trees. That all must be done before any construction on the hotel building could be started. He chided himself for his uneasy feelings, because he had no connection to that house. Sure, he'd thought it to be a lovely structure, but it was in the exact spot where the hotel would be constructed.

Shortly before arriving in Savannah, Shaun's head began throbbing. *Just what I don't need today—a bad headache.* Once he immersed himself in the actual plans of the project and thought about how proud his father would be, Shaun would stop dwelling on memories of Sadie's changed mood at the café. After all, he'd not done or said anything to upset her, and she hadn't mentioned the house that would be demolished.

Grabbing his bags to exit the train upon arrival in Savannah, Shaun drew in a deep breath. He knew the truth was he had an important job to do. If George O'Leary was ever going to be truly proud of his son, then Shaun must focus on his tasks and follow through with outstanding results. Even if that meant not furthering his relationship with Sadie Perkins.

Chapter Six

Pastor Lucas entered the Perkins' cottage the following Saturday morning, clasping a sheaf of papers and beaming at Sadie. "Things are looking more definite. It appears the Lord is working quickly on this."

Sadie's pulse raced as she led the pastor to her kitchen table, where he could spread out the papers and discuss details with her. In a way, she felt this was all a dream, and she'd awaken to realize she wasn't going to be a missionary after all.

But no, this was all very real. She sat across from her pastor, her eyes glancing back and forth from his face to the papers on the table between them. She'd already poured them each a cup of lemonade and hoped the tart liquid would keep her fully alert. The pastor was sharing details that were vital—not to mention exciting.

Details of taking a boat from the small Riverview port to the larger Savannah port had been written on one paper, with more information regarding the ship she would sail on across the Atlantic Ocean to Africa.

Africa! This is really going to happen. Sadie drew in a

shaky breath and noticed Pastor Lucas eyeing her.

"Are you okay? Am I giving this information too quickly? I know it's a lot to take in all at once, but I knew you'd be eager to learn details of what I've arranged for you. If you have any questions or you're not agreeable with any of this, please stop me and we'll discuss it." The middle-aged man's kind expression threatened to bring tears to Sadie's eyes.

"No sir, it all sounds perfectly worked out. I am amazed that you've done all this for me. I'm sure making these arrangements has taken a lot of your time, and you have enough duties as the pastor of our Riverview Church." Sadie took another sip of the lemonade. She was thankful for all her pastor had done to help her.

He smiled and shook his head. "Nonsense. Helping someone prepare for the mission field is one of the most important duties I can do as a pastor. Not to mention it's an honor and privilege for me to assist you in these arrangements. Just think of the lives you'll touch in Africa. The least your church family can do is offer any financial support we can and keep praying for you. And as the pastor I'm more than happy to handle the travel details."

Pastor Lucas pointed to a calendar he'd brought along, then turned to the month of July. Pointing to a small block on the grid, he said, "This is the actual date you'll be leaving for your new life."

She held back a gasp. July! They were already in mid-May, and July wasn't far off. Was she ready for this? It seemed to be happening so quickly. Her head swam, and she took another sip of the tart liquid.

"I felt certain you would be pleased to have a definite departure date, especially so your father will know, and also Mrs. White at the library. When I stopped in a few days ago and spoke with her, I could tell she's supportive of your mission work. Although she admitted she'll miss you terribly." His kind smile flashed again.

Sadie's eyes burned with unshed tears, and she blinked rapidly to keep them at bay. To her dismay she was sure the pastor noticed, but to his credit he didn't comment. His tone remained even and he produced another sheet of paper from his packet.

"Here's a list of items you'll need to pack in your trunk. Of course, feel at liberty to add any other items you might need as well." He slid the paper across the table to Sadie.

Drawing in a deep breath, Sadie willed herself to keep her emotions in check. "Pastor Lucas, again I cannot begin to tell you how much I appreciate the financial contributions of our church. I appreciate your hard work in making these arrangements for me. I couldn't even attempt this without your assistance and guidance."

The pastor rose from his chair. "As I said earlier, helping you with this trip is an honor and privilege for me. You're the one doing the real work—or you will be, once you arrive on foreign soil to work with orphans in Africa."

Sadie accompanied him to the door, bidding him good-bye and thanking him yet again.

After the pastor left, Sadie saw him visiting with her father in their yard. How was Papa going to handle Sadie's absence? Although he'd been supportive, Sadie still fretted about her father needing help while she was away. She was certain the pastor was sharing some of the travel details with Horace, and to Sadie's relief her father looked happy.

As she returned to her Saturday chores, her mind was a continent away. Being a missionary in Africa was what she'd been praying about for months, and now it was becoming a reality. Excitement ran through her, but also fear. Much fear.

Putting away the broom, she hurried to her bedroom and grabbed her Bible. When she allowed the fearful thoughts to gain control, she wasn't trusting in the Lord as she should. Moments later Sadie read familiar passages from the Psalms and the book of Isaiah, and a peace calmed her. If sailing to

Africa was the Lord's will, then He would watch over her. Not only her, but also Papa while she was gone. The only way she could ever leave her father to serve as a missionary was by clinging to that truth.

~ ~ ~ ~

As the train rolled along from Savannah towards Riverview, Shaun was filled with a jumble of emotions. He was eager and excited to see Sadie again, yet he was filled with apprehension about the crew arriving to tear down the house on Willow Lane.

It's just a structure, that's all. A structure has no feelings, but must be removed so a new building can be constructed in its place. Shaun's silent talk didn't make him feel any better, so he gazed out the train window at the passing scenery.

A few farms here and there caught his eye. Children played in yards and mothers hung laundry on lines to dry. Families. Isn't that what he wanted, when all was said and done? Yes, he was currently focusing on making his father proud and being a successful businessman. But deep down inside, past the desire to be successful and even past his grief from losing Grace, the truth lay hidden in his heart. Shaun yearned to have a wife and children and live a peaceful life with his own family around him.

The porter came down the aisle at that moment, calling out the next stop. Riverview would be after the upcoming stop, so Shaun estimated about thirty more minutes. He needed to collect his thoughts and establish a plan.

Since it was Monday, Sadie would be working at the library. After Shaun took his bags to the boardinghouse, he'd stop by and say hello. He hoped she'd be in her usual pleasant mood, rather than acting somber and distant. The memory of her abrupt change in mood at their last luncheon date still troubled him.

After his planned visit, Shaun must concentrate on the hotel plans and work towards carrying out the project. It was almost June, and the actual construction needed to get underway soon.

Sadie's face registered surprise when Shaun entered the library. He was relieved she'd greeted him with a smile.

"I just wanted to stop in and say hello, now that I'm back in Riverview. If it's agreeable with you, I would enjoy seeing you sometime this week. We could have lunch again at the café, or perhaps do something different." Although he had no idea what other activity they could do, he was hoping Sadie would agree to continue seeing him.

She nodded, speaking in a soft voice that made Shaun's heart leap with joy. "If you'd like, I could prepare a picnic supper for us on Thursday. We could meet at the park at six o'clock, if the weather is pleasant."

Trying to keep his voice from sounding overly-eager, Shaun grinned. "That would be nice, but I don't want this to be any trouble for you." He paused, relieved when she shook her head.

"It won't be trouble. Just a simple picnic supper." She directed her gaze to a library patron behind him.

Shaun needed to leave so she could return to her work. He said good-bye, then offered a friendly wave to Polly White, who was shelving some books. He was thankful the librarian hadn't hovered around them. Shaun had the feeling that Polly White liked to know what was being said in the library she ran.

His steps were light on the way to the boardinghouse. Now his challenge would be keeping his thoughts on the hotel plans and the work to be done, rather than anticipating a picnic with Sadie in a few days.

On Tuesday, Shaun was scheduled to meet with the head of a construction company located in nearby Darien. Shaun's father had arranged the meeting, which was to be held at the boarding house. Shaun was thankful that Miss Callie was agreeable and even acted pleased that a business appointment would be conducted at her house.

A few minutes after ten o'clock on Tuesday morning, a pudgy man ambled up the sidewalk to the front door of Miss Callie's. Shaun had been sitting in the front room near a window, so he could watch for the man.

"Are you Mr. Davis? I'm Shaun O'Leary." The men shook hands, and the visitor gave an appreciative glance around the room.

"Yes, I'm Harry Davis—please call me Harry. This sure is a nice place you're staying in." He reached up and wiped his brow with a handkerchief.

"Please call me Shaun. And yes, Miss Callie runs a very nice boarding house. I'm thankful to have such a comfortable place to stay while I'm away from my home in Savannah."

At that moment Miss Callie entered the room, smoothing her apron and smiling at Harry Davis. "I thought I heard voices in here. You men feel free to use the dining room table for your meeting, and I'll bring glasses of lemonade right away." She scuttled off to the kitchen.

Shaun was grateful for Miss Callie's hospitality, and was also eager to get down to business. Soon the men were looking over the hotel plans, as they drank lemonade and discussed the property on Willow Lane.

"I'm eager for you to see the property where the hotel will be constructed and also see the house that your crew will be tearing down." Shaun normally walked to the land from the boarding house, but Harry Davis insisted his carriage driver would transport them.

Shaun felt rather silly riding such a brief distance, but Mr. Davis most likely would've been out of breath if they'd walked. Soon they arrived at the land and both men climbed out of the carriage.

To his surprise, Shaun had the same feeling he'd had before when looking at the house. Chiding himself, he pointed out to Mr. Davis the approximate area the hotel would occupy. "I'm hoping to be able to leave as many trees standing as possible. My father feels they will add to the charm of our establishment, especially since it's supposed to be an upscale hotel." Shaun kept his voice calm and even.

Harry Davis remained quiet as Shaun had talked and pointed out specific details. Then he cleared his throat and shook his head. "Sure does seem a shame to demolish such a lovely structure as this house. A shame indeed." He mopped his brow again with his handkerchief.

"Yes, I agree. But tearing down the house is the only way we can have a hotel constructed. This property couldn't possibly accommodate the planned hotel if the house remains standing." Why did Shaun feel defensive? Had Mr. Davis decided he didn't want to handle the demolition job of the house, and the construction of the proposed hotel?

The men circled the property, discussing the hotel's dimensions and various features planned for the establishment. Later the carriage driver returned Shaun to the boardinghouse, then headed to Darien with Mr. Davis. Another meeting was scheduled for the following Monday, with plans for demolition later in the week.

After the evening meal, Shaun returned to his room, perusing the hotel plans and making more notes from his meeting with the construction foreman. Shoving thoughts aside related to the beauty of the house on Willow Lane, Shaun forced himself to concentrate on details and plans for the hotel. Not only would his father be proud of his success with the project, but Shaun would benefit financially. Then he could move out of his parents' home in Savannah, and have a place of his own.

Yet that thought only led to daydreams of a certain chestnut-haired beauty, sharing his home as his wife. Where had that idea come from? But as he continued poring over his notes for the hotel, Shaun had to admit that the idea of sharing his home—and his life—with Sadie Perkins was a pleasant thought. A very pleasant thought indeed.

~ ~ ~ ~

"The voyage has been moved up? Are you certain, Pastor Lucas?" A wide-eyed Sadie gasped from where she stood in her doorway.

He nodded, his eyes downcast. "I just learned this information today and wanted to come over right away and let you know."

She stepped back and gestured him into her home. "Please come in. I'm sorry I appear to have no manners right now, but I'm shocked. And please don't think me disrespectful in questioning you." Flustered, she offered him a cup of water.

"No, thank you. I'm fine. I'm sorry to be the bearer of not-so-good tidings, but knew you needed to know immediately. I've only learned today that the ship sailing to Africa has been re-scheduled to depart on June fifteenth. Which, as you know, is only three weeks away. I'm so sorry, because I know you'd already informed Mrs. White that you would continue working at the library until the end of June. This greatly changes things." Pastor Lucas appeared uncomfortable, and Sadie had a twinge of remorse. She knew none of this was his fault. He was merely the messenger and had already apologized twice. She must be careful so she didn't sound as upset as she felt at the moment. After all, he'd done so much to help her prepare for her mission voyage.

Sadie drew in a deep breath and pasted a smile on her face. "Well, it will all work out, I'm sure. The Lord is in control, and I will need to make certain I complete everything necessary before June fifteenth." She released a chuckle that she hoped sounded sincere—for the pastor's sake.

He stood and gave her a compassionate glance. Pastor

Lucas was the kindest man she knew, besides her papa. "I will be sure and let you know if I hear of any more news regarding your voyage. In the meantime, please know that you have my prayers, and the continued support of your church family as well." He offered a smile before turning to leave.

"Thank you, Pastor Lucas. Even though this news was a bit of a shock, I want you to know I appreciate everything you've done for me." A lump formed in her throat, so Sadie stopped talking and waved good-bye, watching the pastor leave.

Frozen to the floor, Sadie blinked back tears. What good would crying do? She had much to accomplish before leaving in a few weeks. But she dreaded sharing the news with her father that evening.

Aware of something rubbing against her leg, Sadie glanced down to see her beloved cat Moses by her feet. The feline looked up at her as if he knew she was upset. Sadie scooped him up in her arms and sat in the overstuffed chair in the corner of the room. As she nuzzled her face into the cat's soft, silky black fur, Sadie could no longer contain her tears. She let them flow, releasing pent-up emotions that had been building inside.

The financial support and travel details coming together had seemed a sure indication she was meant to serve in the mission field. So why was she now overcome with sadness at leaving her home? She'd known all along it would be difficult to be away from her father and familiar surroundings, including her cats. But now that her departure date had been moved up, it all seemed too much for her. Between her tears and stroking her cat's fur, Sadie offered up a prayer for guidance. She knew that the Lord would give her the strength and peace she needed, but at the moment she felt like a helpless child, lost with no idea which way to turn.

~ ~ ~ ~

The pot of simmering soup filled the cottage with a delightful aroma. Her father would be home from his job within the half-hour, and Sadie wanted to have the meal prepared.

After her good cry earlier, she'd felt better and had forced herself to stay busy. Lifting the pan of cornbread from the hot oven, Sadie drew in a deep breath and again prayed for guidance. She needed to share her news gently with her father and hoped he wouldn't be upset.

A distant rumble of thunder sounded, and she cast a quick look out the kitchen window. Gray clouds covered the earlier sunshine. *How appropriate. The weather matches my mood.*

Hopefully her father would arrive home before a storm began—if a storm was indeed approaching. Often in the coastal areas the weather played tricks on the residents, giving indications that strong winds and rain were headed their way, only to blow over and have the sunshine return.

But this time Sadie felt certain they were in for a storm. At that moment the thunder growled louder, as if echoing her thoughts. To her relief, her father came in the front door a few minutes later, sniffing the air and grinning.

"The meal you've fixed sure smells tasty. I don't know what I'll do when you're off being a missionary." Although his words were spoken in a teasing manner, Sadie cringed, knowing what she had to tell him.

"You'll be fine. I'm sure ladies from our church will be checking on you to make sure you have enough to eat, and you can eat at the Gingham Goose Café now and then."

She set their bowls of soup and the plate of cornbread on the table, along with their cups of water.

Horace offered the blessing for their meal and the pair began eating. Sadie didn't have much of an appetite due to being nervous about her news. But her father was apparently hungry because he consumed spoonfuls of his soup.

After asking about his workday, Sadie waited a few minutes before plunging in with her news. "Pastor Lucas stopped by this afternoon. He didn't stay long, but he had some interesting news for me." She took a sip of water, feeling her throat constricting.

"What kind of interesting news?" Horace paused between bites and eyed his daughter curiously.

Taking a deep breath, Sadie shared what the pastor had told her about the ship sailing earlier than planned. She shook her head and frowned. "I will admit after the pastor left, I was upset, Papa. Very upset. As much as I want to serve the Lord by being a missionary, I didn't know it would happen quite this soon. And you know I'm not eager to be away from you. Or everyone I know in Riverview. Not to mention I still have so much to do in preparation for the voyage, and Polly White needs me to work at the library, and now I'll have to let her know." Her words tumbled out, but at least she didn't become teary again.

To her surprise, Horace chuckled. Holding up a hand, he spoke in a light tone. "Hold on, Sadie girl. You're gettin' ahead of yourself, it seems to me. Now take a deep breath and tell me from the beginnin' what the pastor learned about the ship."

With her heart racing, Sadie knew her father was right. She was getting ahead of herself, and at this rate would collapse before she even boarded the ship for Africa.

In a much slower voice she recounted the details, then paused before continuing. "I know with the Lord's help I'll get everything done, Papa. But right now it just seems like too much. Getting everything ready, finishing my work at the library, and leaving things situated for you here."

"I'll be fine. Your papa should be the least of your concerns. You just let Mrs. White know about the change in the schedule, and then you'll have to stop work sooner than you'd planned. That's all there is to it, and Mrs. White will know this wasn't your doing."

Sadie nodded. "You're right. I-I have to confess that I dreaded telling you about this, because I don't want to leave you."

Papa reached across the table and patted her arm. "You're not leaving me forever. It's only while you go help those orphans in Africa. Then you'll come back home, and me and your cats will be here waiting." He grinned, then held up his now-empty bowl. "Could I please have some more of your soup? This is some of the best you've cooked." He chuckled and rubbed his stomach.

Her father's request for more soup lightened the mood, and Sadie giggled as she hurried to the stove to ladle more soup into Papa's bowl. When she cleaned the kitchen twenty minutes later, Sadie's mind strayed to thoughts of the planned picnic with Shaun on Thursday. Had she seemed forward in suggesting the picnic supper? He'd appeared pleased at the idea. At least that would be a nice distraction for Sadie, even for an hour.

Before climbing into bed that night, she opened her Bible to several familiar verses. Reading the Scriptures soothed her and served as a reminder that things would be okay. Even if it hadn't appeared that way earlier that day.

The verse from Psalms spoke to her even stronger that night. *I will instruct thee and teach thee in the way that thou shalt go.* She'd read that verse numerous times before, but now she clung to it. No matter what lay ahead, the Lord would be with her and guide her.

~ ~ ~ ~

Since Shaun had no office in Riverview, he was thankful Miss Callie allowed him to use her dining room table as a desk. As long as it wasn't time for breakfast or the evening meal, she was agreeable to the arrangement. Shaun found it helpful to spread out his notes and the hotel plans on the large table.

He grinned thinking about the boarding house owner—she could be firm and serious, yet also kind and understanding. Shaun would never want to get on Miss Callie's bad side. He felt certain the woman could deliver a tongue lashing that would make a tough man cringe.

Glancing at his pocket watch, Shaun was surprised at the time—he'd not realized it was so late. He needed to leave to meet Sadie soon, and the very thought caused his pulse to race. Gathering his notes and other papers, Shaun placed everything into his bag and hurried to his room. Since he'd already let Miss Callie know he wouldn't be there for the evening meal, after he deposited the papers safely in his room, he could leave.

Had she forgotten? Shaun arrived at the park but didn't see any sign of Sadie. Hopefully she wasn't ill. He paced back and forth, trying to enjoy the beauty around him. The trees rustled in the late afternoon breeze as the birds chirped their early evening concert.

Then he saw her. Riding her bicycle, with her hair blowing out behind her shoulders, Sadie made a beautiful sight. Resisting the urge to run toward her, Shaun instead walked at a clipped pace.

The small basket on her bicycle handlebars brimmed with food items, and Shaun was amazed that nothing spilled out.

"Hello there. I hope this wasn't trouble for you. When you suggested a picnic, I wasn't thinking clearly about you carrying the food in your basket."

She put on the brakes and smiled at him. "It wasn't trouble. I just had to pedal more slowly than usual so I wouldn't drop any of our meal." Her cheeks held a touch of pink, and even with windblown hair, she still appeared lovelier than ever.

What was wrong with him? Standing like a fool analyzing Sadie's appearance, when he should be assisting her.

"Here, I'm sorry. Let me help you." He held one of her hands as she dismounted from the bicycle and set the kickstand. Then he lifted the small basket, being careful not to spill anything.

"I hope you're not starving, because our meal isn't big. But I tried to put as much as possible into my basket." Her voice sounded apologetic, tugging at Shaun's heart.

"It looks great to me. Thank you for doing this, and I'm glad the weather is nice too." Standing close to her, he could smell faint wisps of a lavender scent. He had the ridiculous urge to embrace her in a hug, and mentally chided himself. Turning his attention to their meal, Shaun helped spread the checked tablecloth and set out the food. Sadie had packed so much in her small basket, and he enjoyed every bite of the sandwich, cookies, and lemonade.

Soon the conversation flowed, with no trace of Sadie's unusual mood. Shaun was still puzzled by their last date and how quickly Sadie had changed. But now she acted as she had other times they'd been together.

"I can't believe it's almost June. Do you have any special plans for this summer?" Shaun swallowed the last sip of his lemonade and wiped his mouth with a linen napkin Sadie had provided. The woman thought of everything.

As soon as the words left Shaun's mouth, Sadie's eyes widened. Why did she appear nervous after his innocent question?

With a half-smile, Sadie said, "I haven't yet mentioned this, but I've been praying for a while about being a missionary. With the assistance of my wonderful pastor and church family, the details are falling into place and I'll be leaving the middle of June to do mission work. I wasn't supposed to leave until July, but recently my pastor visited and said the ship's departure date had been moved up. I'll leave Riverview on June fifteenth." She glanced down and brushed crumbs off the tablecloth, then returned her gaze to Shaun.

Why did he feel he'd just been punched in the gut? The woman sitting next to him was planning to be a missionary, a noble calling. He should be impressed and happy for her. *Impressed, yes. Happy, no.* She was staring at him, awaiting a response.

"A missionary? I had no idea. That's wonderful." His flat tone didn't match his words at all. He forced a smile on his face, but was a lousy actor. "I know I don't sound very happy for you, but this is a shock. You mentioned a ship, so where are you going?" Shaun wasn't sure he wanted to know the answer. The truth was—he didn't want Sadie to leave Riverview.

"I'm supposed to travel to Africa and work with orphans there. I won't know specific details until I arrive on the continent, which is scary. But that's my heart's desire. I feel led to work with young children and teach them about Jesus." She paused and drew in a shaky breath. "I'm sure there will be many other jobs for me to perform while there, and I'm certain it will be a challenge. I've never been far from home." There was a wistfulness in her tone, and she lowered her eyes, her long lashes contrasting against her smooth skin.

Shaun was still reeling from this news, but very well couldn't act dismayed. "How long will you be in Africa? Or do you know yet?" He regretted not having any lemonade left, as his throat was parched.

"The plan is for a year. That seems like a long time right now, but I'm sure once I arrive and begin working with children, the time will pass quickly." She moistened her lips. Lips that Shaun hadn't yet had a chance to kiss.

Sadie smoothed strands of hair away from her face. "This is something I've prayed about for some time. I've spoken with my pastor, and he's been helpful, advising me and making arrangements. Since I will have to travel by ship, that requires a fairly large sum of money. Many members of my church congregation have helped financially, for which I am extremely grateful. With everything working out so well, it seems this is what I'm meant to do." Sadie clamped her lips together, as though afraid she'd been talking too much.

Shaun reached over and patted her arm. "It does sound as though the details are working out for you. I'm sure the children you work with will adore you, and you'll be missed in Riverview, I feel certain." Another thought formed in his mind. "How does your father feel about this?"

Her reply was accompanied by a bittersweet smile. "He wants me to follow the Lord's leading, and Papa says if this is what I'm called to do, then I need to go. But I know he will miss me, and I'll miss him terribly." Tears pooled in her eyes.

Shaun didn't want her to cry, so he offered a suggestion. "How about if we get up and take a little walk here in the park? I'm afraid my legs shall become numb if I don't move about." He slowly rose, then helped Sadie stand.

To his relief, she'd blinked away the tears and now gazed up at him with a sweet smile.

"Thank you for listening to me ramble on about my trip. I think a walk right now would be good, too." She smoothed her skirt.

The couple strolled for about fifteen minutes, conversing about Shaun's home in Savannah and Sadie's small garden. After their walk, Shaun assisted with repacking her small basket, then held her bicycle steady as she climbed on.

Before she pedaled away, Shaun placed a quick kiss on her cheek. "I hope I can see you again soon." His voice had a pleading tone.

Sadie smiled, told him good-bye, then pedaled away from the park toward her home.

As Shaun watched her ride away, he couldn't help wondering if Sadie would be leaving his life soon. Not riding away, but sailing away on a ship. That thought made him feel weak as he trudged back to Miss Callie's boardinghouse. After such a delightful picnic, how could his steps and his heart be so heavy?

Chapter Seven

"You had a picnic in the park? Oh, how romantic." Lucy clasped her hands underneath her chin and fluttered her eyelashes, a dreamy smile lingering on her mouth.

Sadie swallowed her sip of tea before she spewed it over the parlor floor. Lucy was such a romantic. It was a good thing that Sadie had only shared about the picnic in the park and didn't mention the quick kiss on the cheek. After all, that meant nothing—simply a friendly gesture. Never mind the fact that Sadie could barely pedal all the way home because her pulse was racing.

"I told him about my planned mission trip, and he said he was happy for me. He did appear shocked when I mentioned it. I suppose he didn't think of a library worker also being a missionary." She giggled, but then froze when she noticed her friend's face.

Lucy's brow furrowed. Sadie knew her best friend well enough to know when the woman was worried.

"What's on your mind?" She leaned closer, concern growing at Lucy's demeanor.

"I know this is selfish of me, but I just can't bear the

thought of you being across the ocean. I know you'll be doing a wonderful thing by helping those pitiful little orphans, and I should only focus on that. But you're my dearest, closest friend. I don't know what I'll do without you." Lucy's blue eyes brimmed with unshed tears. She grabbed a lace handkerchief and brought it up to her sniffling nose.

"What on earth is going on in here, ladies?" Lucy's mother stepped into the parlor, holding a tray with a teapot and treats, but stopped about ten feet away. She stared at both women, a frown creasing her face.

"It's fine, Mrs. Stone. Lucy was mentioning my trip to Africa. We'll miss each other very much, but I'm not going away forever." Sadie reached over and patted Lucy's arm.

After more sniffles accompanied by dabbing at her eyes, Lucy said, "I'm fine, and didn't mean to alarm you, Mother. Thank you for bringing more tea for us." She smiled sweetly at her mother, who'd set the porcelain teapot and a saucer of dainty tarts on the small mahogany table in front of the settee.

"Yes, thank you very much." Sadie smiled at Lucy's mother, who continued staring at the women as if wanting to be certain everything was okay. Then, with an uncertain smile and nod, the older woman turned and exited the room.

Sadie thought it best to change the topic of conversation, so she leaned closer. "Tell me about Matthew. Is there any news? What about his upcoming visit?" Sadie was sure mentioning Lucy's beau would lighten her friend's mood, and she was right.

A now-beaming Lucy chattered about details of the impending visit—when he was expected to arrive in Riverview, the activities she had planned for them, and how excited she was about Matthew's visit.

"I wish he could stay longer, but I'm thankful he's coming here for a few days." Lucy lowered her voice to a whisper. "I think Mother is looking forward to Matthew's visit too, but she's trying not to let on." She giggled and placed a hand to her mouth.

Sadie was happy for her widowed friend and had been praying if it was the Lord's will, a lasting relationship would work out for Lucy and Matthew. Of course, Sadie knew better than to even mention the word *wedding*, because Lucy was likely to get overly excited about what she already had planned. No, better to wait. But it did her heart good to see her best friend so happy.

"I'd better return home and get a good night's sleep. I have many chores I need to accomplish tomorrow." Sadie omitted the part that some of them pertained to her mission trip. She didn't want Lucy to become emotional again.

After a quick hug for her friend, Sadie pedaled her bicycle home. She was thankful there was still daylight, because she made a point of never riding after dark. Even though Riverview was considered a safe area, Sadie had no desire to be out after the sun set.

She had difficulty falling asleep that night, because Lucy's earlier words kept replaying in her mind. Especially her comment about Sadie being across the ocean.

Even though Sadie knew she'd be in another country, with the Atlantic Ocean between herself and home, it hadn't affected her as much as it did now. Niggles of worry and doubts bounced around in her mind. Would she be able to do this? Up until now she'd focused on the actual mission work—her duties and also preparations for the trip. She hadn't thought much about being so far from home. Across the ocean. Those words taunted her as she tossed and turned, finally falling into a deep slumber filled with unusual dreams.

~ ~ ~ ~

Sadie awakened on Saturday morning feeling sluggish. She was thankful it wasn't a day to work at the library, because she'd not rested well at all the night before. Perhaps coffee and a good breakfast would help.

"Are you feelin' poorly this mornin', Sadie girl?" Her father's voice held concern. He eyed her over his coffee cup from his place across the kitchen table.

"I'm fine. I just didn't sleep well last night, even after riding my bicycle to visit Lucy. Usually the exercise and fresh air helps me sleep well." She didn't want her father to worry, so as she served him the bacon and eggs she'd prepared, Sadie changed the subject.

"Will you get some rest today? You've worked so hard at the mill lately, and tomorrow we'll have church. Are you staying home today?" She finished serving their plates, then sat across from Papa.

After offering up a blessing for their food, Horace winked at his daughter. "I'll get some rest. After I help the pastor and some other fellars at the church. Pastor Lucas has asked for help with a few repairs on the building, so I figure I can at least offer to work." He shoveled the eggs into his mouth.

Sadie shook her head. "That's kind of you. But please be careful and don't hurt your shoulder. You do enough work at the mill five days a week." She didn't want her father to think she was nagging, so she didn't comment further on the matter, but began eating her eggs and bacon.

While drying the dishes a little later, Sadie's mind drifted to her previous night's visit with Lucy. Thinking of her friend's comment about being across the ocean made Africa seem so far away. *Don't dwell on the distance. Think about those precious children who need to hear about Jesus.* Sadie's silent talk helped a little, but she planned to read her Bible as soon as her chores were finished. Doubts eating away at her would only rob her of energy. With her departure date less than a month away, Sadie needed all the energy she could muster.

The next morning after church several older members

approached Sadie, smiling and offering encouraging comments about her mission work. She felt certain some of those people were also the ones who'd contributed financially to help her, so she tried to exude enthusiasm. After all, who wanted to pay money to assist someone who acted downcast?

Mrs. Lucas bustled up to Sadie and her father at the church doors. "The pastor and I would be honored if you both would join us for Sunday dinner. The meal should be ready by two o'clock, if that's agreeable with you." She looked back and forth from Horace to Sadie, awaiting a reply.

Sadie couldn't help noticing that her father appeared pleased with the invitation. "That would be nice, if you're certain it won't be trouble. And I'll be happy to bring something." Already thoughts of food prepared by Mrs. Lucas were causing Sadie's stomach to rumble—the woman was an excellent cook.

"No trouble at all, and you don't need to bring a thing. Except your father." Mrs. Lucas giggled like a schoolgirl and winked at Sadie, then reached out and patted Horace's arm.

Sadie's father appeared to relish the bit of attention. Hopefully church members would look after him while she was in Africa. It would ease her mind knowing that friends were inviting Papa for meals now and then.

At two o'clock Sadie and her father arrived at the pastor's home, greeted by aromas of Mrs. Lucas's mouth-watering roast and potatoes. Since the gracious woman had insisted that Sadie not bring a thing, Sadie planned to wash the dishes for Mrs. Lucas. It was the least she could do.

During the meal, conversation flowed around the table, with the pastor sharing stories of his younger days attending a school up north. Then he commented on the proposed hotel to be built in Riverview. Shaking his head, he spoke in a serious tone. "It is very surprising that a resort-type hotel would be built in our humble town. I only hope the motive behind it is not greed. In the book of First Timothy, the Bible tells us that the love of money is the root of all evil."

A strange sensation ran through Sadie. She didn't want to share that a man she'd grown fond of was heading up that hotel project, nor did she want to express her dismay that it was to be built on the property of her beloved dream house. No, best to keep her comments neutral, so she turned to Mrs. Lucas and complimented the roast.

The pastor's wife blushed. "I'm thrilled you're enjoying it, dear. It's my pleasure to cook for appreciative folks."

After the meal ended, Sadie prepared to wash the dishes, but the pastor and his wife insisted she look over more information with Pastor Lucas. "Planning for your mission work is much more important than these dishes, Sadie. I appreciate your offer of help, but I'll take care of these. The pastor has some details he wants to discuss. And your Papa is welcome to join you and the pastor." She gestured toward the front room, where Pastor Lucas and her father already sat.

Why was she nervous? Fear of the unknown, most likely. At least she hoped that's all it was. She took her seat at a small table, where the pastor had already spread out several papers. Her father pored over the information.

Pastor Lucas had enlisted the help of a missionary friend and had been able to determine the exact location where Sadie would be stationed, at least for her first few months in Africa. The pastor spoke gently. "I know your heart's desire is to work with orphans, and that's where you'll be after you arrive. It's a home that houses approximately forty children, and you'll be teaching them and doing various jobs at the home. How does this sound to you?"

She thought her heart might burst. Excitement and fear battled for control of her emotions. She hoped neither the pastor nor her father noticed her trembling hands. "This sounds exactly like what I've been praying to do. I cannot thank you enough for all of your help." She paused and looked at her father, who appeared thoughtful.

"What do you think?" Her voice was timid, and to her dismay, tears threatened behind her eyelids.

Horace nodded slowly and rubbed his whiskered chin. "Sadie girl, if this is what you feel the Lord has called you to, then it sounds right. I won't lie and say I'm happy about my girl sailing across the ocean, but as you've reminded me, it's not forever. So I won't interfere with what the Lord says to do." His eyes misted.

It took all of Sadie's strength and will to remain composed. Hearing her father's voice and seeing his brimming eyes threatened to send her into a sobbing fit. She inhaled some ragged breaths to steel herself.

As though sensing what was going on in Sadie's mind, the pastor gathered the papers and stood. "Okay, let's head back to the kitchen and enjoy some pie. My wife has baked one of her apple pies with extra cinnamon. What is left will be sent home with you." He chuckled and motioned for Sadie and her father to precede him to the kitchen.

Neither Sadie nor Horace mentioned her mission work for the remainder of that day. But before going to bed that evening, Sadie looked over the papers from the pastor and felt her pulse racing. Was she doing the right thing? Had she indeed been called to Africa to work with orphans? But what concerned her most was why she was having all these doubts as her voyage drew nearer. Perhaps she was being tested, and if that was the case, she must pray even more.

~ ~ ~ ~

The restless feelings were going to drive him crazy. Shaun was more than eager to get on with the demolition of the house on Willow Lane, then have the land cleared so hotel construction could commence.

Yet deep in his heart, he knew the real reason for his restless feelings. He yearned to see Sadie again, and even more, he wanted her to stay in Riverview rather than leave for Africa. It made no difference that the couple hadn't known each other long at all. Shaun was falling for her, and the more time he spent with Sadie made him long to see her more.

Monday arrived, and Shaun walked over to the property to ensure he was there ahead of Mr. Davis and his crew. When they didn't arrive, he wondered if they'd run into some kind of obstacle on their way from Darien. Certainly not bad weather, because a quick glance at the sky showed a clear day. Darien wasn't far away, so it was unlikely their weather would be different from Riverview's weather.

Shaun paced the sidewalk in front of the property. Instead of feeling excited and imagining the hotel standing proudly on the land before him, all he could see was the house that already stood there. Why did that bother him so? He paced some more, striving to focus on the plans the architect had drawn, thinking how lavish the establishment would be once completed. Not to mention how proud his father would be with Shaun's work on this major project.

A sound grabbed his attention. Shaun jerked up his head. An approaching carriage, and from what he could see, there was only the driver and one passenger. What was going on?

The carriage driver pulled up next to the sidewalk and he nodded at Shaun. An unfamiliar man hopped out of the carriage, obviously nervous as he gestured with his hands.

"Are you Mr. O'Leary? Mr. Shaun O'Leary?" The man appeared to be close to Shaun's age, and his eyes flitted from Shaun to the property and back to Shaun's face.

"Yes, I'm Shaun O'Leary. And you would be—?"

"I'm Clarence Horton, and Mr. Davis sent me. He's been taken ill and doesn't know when the construction crew will be able to arrive. He sends his deep regrets, but as I said, he's ill." The man stopped speaking, took a long look at the house, then peered at Shaun.

"Is that the house to be torn down by Mr. Davis's crew?"

His eyes widened.

"Yes, that's right. And I'm sorry that Mr. Davis is ill, but does he not have an assistant who can oversee the crew? I'm eager for the work to begin, and the hotel cannot be built until this house is demolished and the land is cleared." Shaun knew he was scowling, but he couldn't hide his irritation at the moment.

Clarence Horton looked embarrassed and apologetic. With a slow shake of his head he replied, "No, Mr. O'Leary, I'm sorry to say that Mr. Davis is the only one in charge for the company. We're all hoping he recovers soon, because with no jobs being done, no one gets paid." Mr. Horton clamped his mouth shut as if afraid he'd said too much.

Shaun rubbed the back of his neck and released a sigh. "So you don't have any idea when the work here can be started? It all depends on when Mr. Davis recovers, is that correct?" Clarence Horton was only the messenger and the situation wasn't his fault, but in his current mood Shaun felt the urge to throttle someone.

As though sensing Shaun's growing irritation, Mr. Horton scurried back into the carriage and nodded at Shaun. "That is correct. We are sorry for the inconvenience, but as soon as Mr. Davis is well, he will be in touch with you. Good day, sir." He nudged the carriage driver and they continued on down Willow Lane.

While the carriage drove out of sight, Shaun suppressed the sudden urge to scream. Instead he kicked at a rock on the ground, and then another. Now what was he supposed to do? His father had entrusted this project to him, and he couldn't even complete the first major step. At least he had met with the architect and had the hotel plans ready, but what good were the plans if construction couldn't begin?

With one more glance at the house, which now seemed to be mocking him, Shaun stormed back toward Miss Callie's. As he drew nearer to the boardinghouse, he changed his direction. He knew exactly where he'd go and whom he would see. Surely his day would get better.

~ ~ ~ ~

After Sadie agreed to meet him the following day at the café, Shaun's mood was lighter as he exited the library. Visiting Sadie on a whim resulted in a brief—but pleasant—talk and he anticipated spending time with her on Tuesday.

He had intentionally not shared anything about his meeting with Clarence Horton—after all, Sadie was at her job and Mrs. White hovered nearby, so Shaun kept the conversation casual. But he planned to tell her about it when they met for lunch. She'd be a sympathetic listener and perhaps even say something to boost his present glum outlook on the hotel situation.

That afternoon Shaun mulled over his notes on the construction project. He almost laughed out loud at himself. *What construction project? You can't even get the house torn down to begin building the hotel.* The silent voice in his head mocked him, and he ended up grabbing his notes and papers and thrusting them into his satchel.

"Having a rough day?" Miss Callie came into the dining room, apparently ready to prepare the table for the evening meal. Shaun decided it was just as well he'd already gathered up his papers.

Shaun forced a polite smile. "Some business plans didn't get completed this morning, so I've been feeling frustrated. But I'm sure things will look brighter soon." Rising from the table, he carried his satchel to his room. He attempted to read for a while, but had difficulty staying focused. Soon the aromas from Miss Callie's kitchen drifted to his room, and even without looking at his watch Shaun knew it must be almost six o'clock.

The meal was delicious as always, and Shaun discovered he was hungrier than he'd thought earlier. The slices of ham, the green beans, and Miss Callie's feather light biscuits were like a soothing balm after his frustrating day.

The next day, Shaun arrived at the Gingham Goose Café and secured a table in one corner, hoping for as much privacy as possible. He was more than a little eager to see Sadie, although he'd seen her briefly the day before.

He didn't have to wait long, because Sadie soon entered the café, looking radiant in her mint green dress. As Shaun seated her, he caught a faint whiff of the lavender fragrance she always wore. So feminine and light, just like the woman seated across from him.

Before he shared details of his disappointment from the previous day, he wanted to hear about her mission trip. Although he preferred not to think about Sadie leaving Riverview, he was determined to spend as much time as possible with her before she left.

As they ate their bowls of soup and cornbread muffins, Sadie gave a few details about her upcoming trip. At this point the trip was inevitable—especially after Sadie told him about her recent meeting with her pastor.

"It sounds as though your pastor has been very helpful."

"Oh yes, I couldn't have gotten this far if not for Pastor Lucas. After he realized I was serious about pursuing my dream of being a missionary, he went beyond in helping me." She took a sip of her soup.

"Has that always been your dream? Becoming a missionary?" He was determined to learn as much as possible about the beautiful woman, and knew he was running out of time. Of course, he realized that would make him miss her even more after she left. But for now, he wanted to get to know Sadie Perkins.

After hearing his question, Sadie averted her eyes, as though lost in thought. A few moments of silence hung in the air. Had his question upset her?

When she replied, it was in a soft voice. Her tone was wistful. "No, being a missionary has not always been my dream." There was uncertainty in her eyes. "But I have always yearned to work with children." She clamped her lips closed. It was obvious she didn't want to say more, so Shaun didn't press.

"What about your work? Do you enjoy working with your father in the real estate business?" Sadie took a sip of her water, her emerald green eyes gazing at him over the goblet.

Shaun grinned, hoping to sound convincing where his father was concerned. "Yes, I do—at least most of the time. This current project is my biggest challenge yet, because my father is allowing me to handle the majority of the details." He finished the last of his water before continuing. "But yesterday was not a good day, I'm sorry to say. I hope when I stopped by the library to see you that I didn't appear in a foul mood." He chuckled.

Sadie's head tilted to one side. "No, you didn't. What happened yesterday with your job?" She seemed interested.

Shaun went on to explain yesterday's happenings—or lack thereof. "I was frustrated when the demolition crew didn't arrive, and then when a company representative showed up to tell me the head of the company was ill and wasn't sure when they would be able to do the job, I was upset. Not at the man being ill, of course. That can't be helped. But the fact that the crew depended on having Mr. Davis with them before they could tear down the house was frustrating, to say the least."

The reaction Shaun expected was not the reaction he received.

A shadow flitted across Sadie's features, and she bristled. No words of sympathy or encouragement came from her mouth. Silence hung in the air. A silence that gave Shaun a strange sense of foreboding.

For the first time, he felt awkward in her presence. What was going on? Why was she staring at him in that manner?

He cleared his throat and spoke again, hoping to evoke some kind of positive response from her. "Anyway, I will either have to locate another construction crew to do the job, or wait until Mr. Davis recovers from his illness. Since his assistant was vague on the nature of the illness, I have no idea how long it will be before the man recovers." The air seemed so thick it could be sliced with a knife. Too bad he'd finished his water. He could use the cool liquid now.

As Sadie remained silent, Shaun asked if she'd like anything else to eat or drink. The tone of her response cemented the fact she was upset. Yet he had no idea why.

"No thank you, I'm full. The lunch was delicious, and I need to be on with my errands." She was preparing to leave.

This wasn't how his time with Sadie was supposed to turn out. What was going on?

"Please wait. Is something bothering you? Have I offended you in some way, or perhaps you don't feel well?" He couldn't imagine anything he'd said or done to offend her, but he was searching for answers to her sudden change in mood. Yet again.

She shook her head and offered him a sad smile. "No, you haven't offended me, and I feel fine. Thank you again for the delicious lunch. Perhaps I'll see you again soon." With that, Sadie left the table, clutching her reticule, and headed outside to her bicycle.

Shaun sat at the small table, feeling numb. She'd told him she needed to take care of her errands.

But as he watched her pedal out of sight, another thought occurred to him, causing his heart to sink even lower. Maybe she only wanted to get away from him. But why?

~ ~ ~ ~

Had she been rude? Sadie pedaled as quickly as possible along the main street of Riverview, knowing she should stop by the store but longing to return home. Her emotions won out, and twenty minutes later she was inside her cottage, sitting with Moses in her lap, mulling over Shaun's words.

How could the man speak about tearing that beautiful house—*her dream house*—as if it was an old tool shed? Didn't he appreciate true beauty and craftsmanship in a structure? After all, the man was in the real estate business, and was supposed to be overseeing a construction project.

That must be the answer. Shaun O'Leary wasn't focusing on the beauty of the house standing on the property—he was intent on clearing the land to have a hotel built in its place. A hotel that would no doubt bring Shaun and his father a great deal of money.

Pastor Lucas's words rang in her memory from the previous Sunday. *The Bible tells us that the love of money is the root of all evil.* There was a tightness in the pit of her stomach, and it had nothing to do with the lunch she'd eaten.

A sudden knock at her front door snapped her from her thoughts, and she lifted Moses from her lap and set him on the floor. She wasn't expecting visitors.

Lucy stood in her doorway, looking pretty as ever in a yellow dress with a matching sunbonnet. Her wide eyes stared at Sadie.

"Come in, Lucy. Are you okay?"

"Yes, but I was going to ask the same of you. I was taking a walk and saw you pedaling your bicycle. You were going unusually fast, as though you were being chased by a dog. I was worried, so came to check on you."

How flushed her friend's cheeks were. Apparently, Lucy had hurried to come and see about her. She was such a devoted friend, but Sadie felt guilty that she'd caused her friend concern.

Ushering Lucy into the kitchen, Sadie insisted her friend sit at the table. After pouring cups of lemonade, Sadie explained what happened at her lunch with Shaun.

"Hearing him speak about tearing down that beautiful house on Willow Lane just broke my heart. Although we'd already heard that's where the hotel will be built, it made it seem so real." She looked down for a moment, then met

Lucy's gaze. "I'm a tad embarrassed now. It was rude of me to thank him for the lunch and then leave the café." She drew in a shaky breath. "But if I continued sitting there as he talked about the demolition crew not showing up, I'd likely start crying. That would've been embarrassing."

Lucy's tone offered comfort. "Don't be hard on yourself. You've always loved that house—especially since you and your mother used to walk past it and talk about it. There's a special meaning attached to the house. Perhaps you should share that with Shaun, and he'll know not to mention the—" Lucy seemed hesitant to utter the word. "The demolition of the house." She gave Sadie a smile.

Whatever would she do without Lucy? Later that day Sadie reflected on her visit with Lucy and she knew her friend was right. Perhaps the next time Sadie was with Shaun, she could tell him how special the house on Willow Lane had always been to her. But at the moment, she'd ride her bicycle over to the house and view it while it was still standing. Who knew how much longer it would be there?

~ ~ ~ ~

After paying for their food in the café, Shaun ambled to Miss Callie's boardinghouse, more confused than ever. What had just happened at the table with Sadie? Everything had been going well until he shared his frustrating experience with the construction company. He'd expected a sympathetic response, but instead, Sadie's countenance became the opposite. She'd bristled at his comments.

What had he said that caused her to become withdrawn and silent, and rush out of the café? It must have something to do with the house on Willow Lane being torn down, but what? All he knew was at the mention of the demolition, Sadie's mood changed.

After arriving at the boarding house, Shaun reviewed his notes to decide what to do. Should he wait for Mr. Davis to recover from whatever illness the man had, or should he go forward and locate another company to do the demolition? Ultimately, he knew his decision would have to be acceptable with his father. After all, he was still the owner of the real estate company.

Frustrated after perusing the papers spread before him, Shaun decided to take a walk to Willow Lane, where he could view the property yet again. Perhaps a sudden revelation would come to him, and he'd know what to do. *Don't expect that to happen, O'Leary.* The voice in his mind taunted him.

Stepping outside in the afternoon sunshine gave a small boost to his spirits. At least he breathed in the fresh air when he walked, and he enjoyed seeing the different streets in Riverview. Such a charming little town. Hopefully it would be enticing to tourists once the hotel was completed.

Rounding the corner toward Willow Lane, Shaun glanced left and right, taking in yet again the nearby residences located on the street, which were becoming familiar to him. Birds chirped in the tall oak trees, and the faint laughter of children playing reached his ears. Such a peaceful setting should appeal to tourists who preferred to be a short distance from the main area of town.

He stopped short. A person was walking across the yard, heading toward the street. *Sadie!*

Her bicycle leaned against a tree on the property. Apparently, she'd been circling the house. He didn't want to startle her, so he slowed his steps.

At that moment she saw him, then ducked her head. What was going on? Was she hoping he didn't see her?

He quickened his steps until he was running toward her. When he got within an arm's length, she peered up at him. Tears streamed down her cheeks, and she used the back of her hand to swipe at her red, puffy eyes.

Shaun's heart wrenched. Reaching out to gently take hold of her arms, he leaned in closer to her face. "Sadie.

What's wrong? Why are you crying? Please tell me—I've been worried since you left our lunch so quickly today."

She didn't reply, but only shook her head as tears still trickled down her cheeks. With each sniffle, her slender shoulders shook.

A helpless feeling overwhelmed Shaun. Had he done something to cause this? He gave her a few moments to gain composure, continuing to hold her arms. As he gazed into her lovely emerald eyes, he could bear it no longer. He pulled her against his chest. Neither of them spoke a word, but for a few minutes he held her, feeling her distraught body against his.

Reluctantly he let go when she pulled away. Still sniffling but with her crying under control, Sadie looked up at him again.

"I-I'm sorry you're seeing me this way. I didn't know you'd be coming here this afternoon." She reached into her dress pocket and pulled out a lace handkerchief, then dabbed her eyes repeatedly. It was obvious she was embarrassed.

"You don't need to tell me you're sorry. Just please tell me what has upset you so. I care about you and don't want to see you like this. Please tell me." He kept his voice gentle, although he knew his tone was pleading. He might burst if he didn't find out what was going on with her.

Moistening her lips, Sadie nodded and turned to face the house. In a voice so soft Shaun had to strain to hear her words, she explained. "This house has always been very special to me, and even more so since my mother died when I was fifteen." She went on to describe the walks she and her mother took, and how they always stopped and looked at the house. "I used to say this house is where I wanted to live when I grew up, and my mother always told me that perhaps one day I could."

She released a bitter-sounding chuckle and met Shaun's gaze. "This must sound childish and silly to you, but for me it's a big part of my childhood memories. I'd even thought that when I return from serving as a missionary, I might be able to restore this house and—" Her voice trailed off.

Shaun leaned in, his pulse racing. "And what, Sadie?"

"I'd thought perhaps I could open a home for children here. Either an orphanage or a home for neglected children who need a place to live, where someone cares for them." The tears again pooled in her eyes and she sniffed.

Shaun was certain of one thing in that moment. The beautiful woman standing before him had a heart of gold. Unsure of what to say, he took hold of her arms and pulled her into an embrace. She didn't resist, and they stood a few moments sharing a tender moment. An embrace in the yard of the house that Sadie loved, the one he planned to have demolished.

He felt like an ogre. Why hadn't she shared this information with him before? Yet he had to admit it couldn't have made a difference. Shaun's father had determined that this particular property would be the ideal location for a hotel. So why did Shaun feel so terrible, as though his heart was breaking? Looking down at the beautiful woman with the tear-stained face, he knew. Shaun loved Sadie Perkins, and if this house was special to her, then it mattered to him.

Chapter Eight

Sadie was drained—emotionally and physically—upon her return home that afternoon to prepare supper. Although she had no appetite whatsoever, she needed to have a meal ready for her father. She also needed to act as though it had been a normal day.

Normal day? Hardly. After Lucy visited, Sadie rode her bicycle to the house on Willow Lane, never suspecting she'd be overcome with emotion and then Shaun O'Leary would show up.

Thinking of Shaun again made her pulse race—in a good way. Not only was the man handsome and kind, he actually cared about her. When he'd embraced her, twice, it felt so wonderful and warm. She could've lingered there much longer.

Her face blushed at the thought. What was wrong with her? She was meant to remain single and be a missionary. Even after her mission work in Africa was finished, she'd continue to live her life as a single woman serving the Lord. So why was she relishing thoughts of a man hugging her and caring about her?

She had to admit the truth to herself. Sadie cared about Shaun. A lot. Since she was sailing to Africa in less than a month, this was not good. It would only make her departure more difficult. After all, she'd already been dreading saying good-bye to her papa and Lucy, not to mention all the other folks in Riverview who were special to her. She didn't need to add an attractive man into the mix.

Sadie was more confused than ever, so after putting a pot of stew on to simmer, she headed to her favorite chair and grabbed her Bible off the small table. Turning to the book of Psalms, Sadie read several of her favorite verses that reminded her of the Lord's guidance. If she could only focus on the truth of these verses rather than allowing doubts and worry to take over.

Horace limped through the door a few minutes later.

"Papa, did you work too hard at the mill today? Please sit at the table and I'll serve your stew." She didn't want to verbalize to him how exhausted he appeared.

After washing his hands, her father sat down and released a sigh. "I'm fine, Sadie girl. We've just been a mite busy at the mill, which is really a good thing. And I'm thankful for my job and a nice house to come home to each day. Not to mention my kind daughter fixin' my meals." He grinned at her before taking a gulp of his water.

Hearing her father mention the daily meals, Sadie's heart tugged. Would Papa would have enough to eat while she was in Africa? Sadie shoved the worry away, reminding herself of the Scripture she'd read before her father arrived home. If the Lord continued guiding her into the mission field, then Sadie had to trust that her father would be fine while she was away. But sometimes trusting rather than worrying was hard to accomplish, so she'd better keep praying for guidance and strength.

~ ~ ~ ~

Shaun sat at Miss Callie's dining room table the next day, papers and notes spread out before him. He dropped his head in his hands and released a sigh. There had to be another way. Could the hotel be constructed without tearing down the house on Willow Lane? At the moment the thought seemed impossible, but he had to do something.

After seeing Sadie's tear-streaked face and hearing why the house had such special meaning to her, Shaun couldn't even think about demolishing the structure. But what could be done? His father's company had purchased the property, including the house, for the sole intent of constructing a hotel. Plans had been drawn up and George O'Leary was depending on Shaun to follow through with the project.

What would his father say if Shaun explained how special the house was to Sadie? *He would laugh at you and question your mental stability.* The voice answering in his mind only served to make Shaun feel more miserable. And confused. He had a job to do, yet in carrying through with it, he'd be doing something devastating to the woman he loved.

Loved? The thought jolted through him like lightning, yet he couldn't deny it. Yes, he loved Sadie Perkins. It didn't matter that he'd not known her long. He loved everything about her—the way she looked at him, her soft voice and gentle mannerisms, and her golden heart. Wanting to help orphans in Africa, and then returning home to care for needy children here in the Riverview area. Totally selfless—unlike any woman he'd ever met. All of those qualities in addition to Sadie being the loveliest female he'd ever seen.

What could he do? If he was a praying man, he'd pray. But God didn't have time for him. After Grace had died, Shaun's anger took over and he'd turned away from God. He had no right to ask anything of God now.

"This telegram just arrived for you." Miss Callie burst into the dining room, pulling Shaun out of his private musings and startling him at the same time. A telegram?

"Thank you. And again, I appreciate your being so kind

about allowing me to use your table to do my work—it's been a tremendous help for me." He smiled at the older woman, noticing a slight blush on her wrinkled face.

"No trouble at all. Besides, you always have your papers gathered up before I serve a meal, so it works out fine." She glanced at the telegram Shaun now held in his hands. "I sure hope that's not bad news." A worried frown creased her brow as she turned toward the kitchen.

"Thank you." Shaun turned his full attention to the note. It was from his father, and Shaun saw right away it was related to business.

His eyes skimmed the message, then he read it again. He should've known his father would be eager to learn of progress on the hotel. George O'Leary's telegram simply stated that he hoped Shaun was moving forward on the hotel, and the demolition had been completed as planned. His note added that he hoped construction had begun.

After reading the note for the third time, Shaun felt he'd been punched in the gut. What was he going to do now? His temples were beginning to throb, matching the rhythm of the distant rumbling of thunder. A storm to match his mood—how appropriate.

Rising from the table, Shaun paced the dining room. If one of the other boarders had seen him at that moment, they'd surely think he was going mad. Perhaps he was, because he was beginning to question his own sanity.

Forcing himself to breathe deeply, Shaun sat down again at the table. He must put things in perspective. Sadie would be leaving for Africa in a matter of days, so she wouldn't be in town to see the house she loved being torn down, then replaced with a hotel. By the time she returned from her mission work, she'd be so consumed with helping orphans that thoughts of the house on Willow Lane would only be a memory for her.

Shaun gathered up his papers along with his father's telegram and placed them in his satchel. He needed some fresh air. Shaun glanced at his watch and saw he had plenty of time before Miss Callie served the evening meal. Thankfully the thunder he'd heard earlier had stopped, and sunshine peeked through the clouds. Leaving the boarding house, Shaun headed toward the business district of Riverview. He had a desire to see the water, so he turned his steps in the direction of the small port.

Fifteen minutes later Shaun was strolling along the dock, taking in the sights and marine smells around him. The warm, humid air seemed to envelop him, but rather than being stifling, it was somehow comforting. He'd enjoyed strolling near the river in Savannah when he was a boy, and that old feeling returned to him. Gradually a peace washed over him as he gazed at the Altamaha River.

He wasn't sure of any details, but Shaun now felt the entire situation would work out. As he continued gazing out at the water, a longing came over him. A longing to see Sadie again. He needed to see her and talk with her, because the days were slipping by. She would be on a ship to Africa before he knew it.

~ ~ ~ ~

Lucy stepped into the library, radiant in a pale blue dress that brought out her eyes. She smiled at Sadie, who was busy shelving books.

"I don't want to disturb you while you're working, but Matthew will be arriving in a few days. Mother had a splendid idea to have a nice dinner on Saturday, and we want you and your father to attend. Nothing fancy, just the six of us. But this will be a chance for Matthew to get to know the special people in my life in an informal way." Lucy finally paused to take a breath and slipped a small paper fan from her dress pocket. As she began fanning her face, she giggled. "I'm getting so excited about seeing him again. Please say you and your papa will be there."

Sadie grinned. "Yes, we'll be there. And please tell your mother if there's anything I can bring to let me know. I'm honored we've been invited." Another thought occurred to Sadie. "Besides, I worry about my papa working too hard, so this will be a good opportunity for him to relax and enjoy visiting with your father."

Lucy readily agreed, then said good-bye before hurrying out the door.

Sadie stood for a few moments watching her best friend leave. She was reminded yet again how blessed she was having Lucy in her life, but it also hit her how much she'd miss her while in Africa.

Shoving those thoughts from her mind, Sadie focused on happy thoughts of Lucy and Matthew—how wonderful it would be if a lasting relationship worked out for them. Sadie would be thrilled and knew without a doubt Lucy would be too.

Lost in thought, she barely heard the library door open again, but didn't miss Polly White clearing her throat. Sadie glanced at the librarian, then at the door.

Shaun entered, looking handsome as ever. No wonder Polly had a smile on her face. Sadie's boss hadn't made any secret of the fact she thought Shaun was a charming man.

A hesitant smile formed on Sadie's lips, mixed emotions whirling through her. She hadn't expected to see him again so soon. Sliding the last book into its place on the shelf, Sadie turned and strode toward him. "Hello, Shaun."

He'd already nodded at Polly White, and now turned his full attention on Sadie. "Hello. I hope I'm not interrupting your work." His hands fidgeted and his eyes darted around the room. Nerves? Or perhaps it was her imagination.

She shook her head, then led the way over to a window so they could talk for a few minutes. After the events of the previous day, Sadie didn't want to be within earshot of the librarian.

"I wanted to check on you today and see when we could

have another outing. I really need to talk to you. I know you're leaving for Africa soon, so I didn't want to wait." His voice sounded urgent.

Sadie nodded and attempted to keep her tone casual. "Yes, I'll be departing in only two weeks. But I do have some free time. Are you heading back to Savannah soon?" Perhaps that's why he was so eager to see her again.

He shrugged. "Well, I'm not planning to, but it will depend on my father. If he needs to discuss business plans in person, then I'll have to catch a train and return. But I'll be back in Riverview before you leave for Africa."

Sadie didn't want to suggest a time for them to meet. She'd much prefer Shaun take the lead, so she waited.

"Would you be able to meet for dinner this evening? I'll let Miss Callie know I won't be at the boarding house, and we can eat at the café, if that's agreeable to you. You certainly don't have to ride your bicycle. I can pick you up in a carriage."

Sadie decided that might be a nice change. "That would be delightful. What time shall I be ready?"

"Is six o'clock okay with you?"

"Yes, I'll be watching for you. Shall I write the address?"

He grinned and shook his head. "No, I remember where you told me you live. I'll see you at six." He touched her arm and gave it a light squeeze, then turned to exit the library. Before leaving he said good-bye to Polly White. It amused Sadie to see her boss blush.

Before Sadie could continue with her work, Polly bustled over to her.

"Oh, that man is so nice and polite. He'd make a good catch for some young lady." The librarian's face turned pink, but embarrassment didn't prevent her from speaking. "In fact, I've noticed a little spark between the two of you." She ducked her head as soon as the words left her mouth.

Sadie was taken aback by Polly's boldness. The woman

was outspoken about certain matters, but Sadie had never heard her say anything so personal—especially relating to romance.

Unsure what to say, Sadie smiled and tried to keep her voice calm. "He's a nice man, as you said. But we haven't known each other long. And I'll be leaving soon for my mission work." Although she tried to keep her tone light, her voice carried a wistfulness.

Polly offered a sad smile. "I know, dear. And while I'm so proud of you for following through on your dream of being a missionary, I will admit I'll miss you." She released a sniff, then whirled around to the counter where a patron was waiting.

Sadie had no idea the librarian felt so emotional about her leaving. It touched Sadie to know the woman cared that much, but also added to the doubts tumbling through her mind. Already in one day she had been reminded that she'd be leaving behind Lucy and Shaun, and now even her boss had made it clear she'd miss Sadie. And yes, she would miss Polly also.

When she first began working in the library, Sadie had to get used to the often-serious librarian, who spoke her mind at times. But gradually, she'd seen the softer side of the woman. Polly White had a tender heart under that tough exterior.

A few minutes later the librarian approached Sadie again, this time grinning. "I'm not prying, but since Mr. O'Leary visited you earlier, do you perhaps have plans to see him later today?"

Sadie could barely keep from bursting out laughing, as she was sure the woman had discreetly eavesdropped on their conversation. "Yes ma'am. He's picking me up in a carriage and we'll have dinner at the Gingham Goose Café."

The older woman's eyes lit up. "Then you need to leave here a few minutes early, so you can go home and get ready for Mr. O'Leary. We're not busy here today, so I insist you leave a little before five o'clock. That way you'll have time to prepare your father's meal before you're picked up." The woman thought of everything.

"That's very kind. If you're certain it won't be a problem." She wondered if her boss was about to shoo her out the door at that moment.

Sure enough, at fifteen minutes before five o'clock, Polly White cleared her throat and bade Sadie good-bye.

While pedaling home, Sadie was filled with curiosity about what Shaun wanted to discuss with her. Had he decided not to tear down the house on Willow Lane? No, she couldn't let her thoughts venture there. He had a job to do, which was to oversee the construction of a hotel. He couldn't begin that until the house was gone.

Once again, her eyes misted as she thought about that beloved house and her childhood memories of taking walks with her mother. But a tugging at her heart let her know that wasn't the only reason her eyes filled with tears. She'd be leaving her home soon—her father and everyone she loved. Including a man she hadn't met that long ago, but who'd captured her heart.

~ ~ ~ ~

Shaun was more than a little relieved he'd had no difficulty arranging for a carriage on such short notice. He'd assured the driver he would receive a generous tip, and the wiry man appeared pleased.

Even though the Gingham Goose Café was a comfortable place with tasty food, Shaun wished he was taking Sadie to a fancier place that evening. He could imagine her dressed in a flowing silk gown as he escorted her into a lavish restaurant. Would he ever have an opportunity to do that? Not likely, since she was due to sail out in two weeks. His pulse raced at the thought.

When he'd told Miss Callie he wouldn't be at the

boarding house for the evening meal, she'd teased him about having a dinner date with one of Riverview's lovely ladies. Could she be aware he was seeing Sadie Perkins? It wouldn't surprise Shaun—after all, Riverview was a small town, and talk traveled fast. If Miss Callie did know, that was fine.

Now he stepped onto the front porch of the neat cottage where Sadie lived with her father. Wicker chairs sat on the porch, flanked by pots of colorful spring flowers. Obviously a woman's touch, he mused as he knocked lightly on the door.

A middle-aged man opened the door, inviting him inside.

Shaun was glad to meet Sadie's father, and the man seemed kind and down-to-earth.

A delightful aroma wafted through the air, and Shaun supposed that Sadie had prepared a meal for her father since she'd be dining with him that night. She was truly a devoted daughter.

Entering the room, Sadie greeted Shaun with a smile, then placed a quick kiss on her father's weathered cheek. "I won't be late, Papa. And if you decide you want some pudding, it's in the icebox." She grinned at her father.

Horace Perkins patted his stomach. "Sadie girl, I'm still mighty full from that delicious soup you prepared for me. Now you two have a nice time eating together. Looks like our weather is holding good, so you shouldn't get any rain fallin' on you."

Shaun again shook hands with Sadie's father, expressing his pleasure in meeting the man. And he meant it. Although this was his first time meeting Horace, he liked the man right away.

As the couple rode along the Riverview streets in the carriage, Sadie appeared to be enjoying herself, almost reminding Shaun of a young child doing something adventurous.

"I know you enjoy riding your bicycle, but isn't this a nice change from your usual habit?" He teased her and got the result he'd hoped for.

"Yes, it is. Thank you for obtaining a carriage and driver for us. I hope it wasn't too much trouble."

He assured her it was his pleasure. They entered the café. Relieved to see their usual table empty, Shaun ushered Sadie over and helped her get seated. "I really like this café, but I must admit I'd enjoy taking you somewhere...um, fancy." He grinned, hoping his comment didn't make him sound snobbish. Sadie would likely be shocked at how wealthy his family was, so he'd tried to guard some of his comments.

She giggled. "This café is fine. I daresay I wouldn't know how to act in a fancy establishment." She perused the menu, then closed it as their server appeared.

Unsure whether to wait until after they'd eaten to broach the subject of the house, Shaun took a deep breath and plunged in. "I don't want you to become upset by my mentioning the house on Willow Lane again. But please hear me out. Now that I know how much the house means to you, I'm trying to determine if there's any way the hotel can be constructed on the property without tearing down the house. After all, that piece of land is several acres."

He tried to gauge her reaction to his words, but couldn't tell what was going through Sadie's mind. Her expression was thoughtful, but she remained silent.

"Anyway, I've given it a lot of thought since yesterday, and I'll need to discuss it with my father, since he's the primary owner of our company. I've even thought about suggesting to him that we purchase another piece of land for the hotel, but I can only imagine what his reaction would be. Especially since the purchase of this property has been finalized." Shaun shook his head and hoped he wasn't making his father sound like a tyrant.

He wanted Sadie to say something—something that

would show she understood his dilemma. This was a business situation, after all, and he was trying to work things out in Sadie's favor. He took a sip of his water, still studying her face.

She looked at him with a bittersweet smile. "I appreciate what you're trying to do. And I appreciate that you understand how—and why—that house is so special to me, even though I have no personal ties to it. I've never had relatives or friends who resided there, only the memories of walking past with my mother and daydreaming about it." She paused, her eyes misting, but to Shaun's relief, no tears streamed down her pretty face as they'd done the day before.

"After the way I behaved yesterday, I was certain you'd think I was being ridiculous. So it means a lot to me that you understand my feelings, and that you're trying to work out a different plan so the house can remain." She released a sigh and her eyes took on a faraway look. "But I don't see how you could leave the house standing and still construct a hotel on that land. Of course, I'm no builder, but it doesn't seem possible."

Their server returned with the meals, so Sadie bowed her head to offer up her blessing as she always did. Shaun remained silent and didn't begin eating until she'd raised her head again.

Before she took a bite of her ham, she added, "But it's kind of you to at least try to leave the house standing."

Deciding it best to keep the conversation light for the remainder of their time together that evening, Shaun asked questions about her library job. He avoided discussing her upcoming mission trip, for fear that would stir up her emotions again.

After their meal was finished, they remained at the table a little longer. Shaun was thankful no other customers were sitting close by, because he wanted to let Sadie how he felt. As though to spite him, a couple sat at the nearest table. A very loud couple, making Shaun glad their meal was done.

"Would you like to ride around in the carriage for a bit? I've got the driver hired until nine o'clock." Shaun grinned, hoping earnestly he'd be able to say what he wanted to share with her.

After paying for their meal, Shaun escorted Sadie to the waiting carriage, then instructed the driver to take them down the least-crowded streets in Riverview. He noticed Sadie looking curious.

Riding along the streets in the carriage proved to be an enjoyable experience, and as the daylight gave way to night, Shaun pointed to stars already twinkling in the sky. Crickets chirped and lights shone from inside houses they passed, adding to the coziness of their ride.

With a start Shaun realized where the driver was taking them. The carriage was headed down Willow Lane. Oh no, this might not be a good idea at all. It certainly had not been Shaun's intention.

He shifted to face Sadie. "I'm sorry, I had no idea our driver would come to Willow Lane. I'll ask him to turn the carriage around and take another street." He squeezed Sadie's hand.

She shook her head. "It's fine. We're taking a carriage ride, and I believe you did request that we not travel the busiest streets. The driver is only following your request." After she gave him a reassuring smile, he blew out a sigh of relief.

Knowing the hovering dusk would soon give way to night, Shaun had to speak or wait until another opportunity. His time was running out. He turned in the carriage seat so he was facing Sadie, then took both her hands in his.

"I realize we haven't known each other very long, but I've already grown to care very much about you. I think it's wonderful you have such a giving, loving heart and want to help orphans. But is your trip to Africa definite? Please forgive me for asking this, but the more I'm around you, the more I don't want to see you go so far away." Was he saying too much? He didn't want to come on too strong and scare her away.

Sadie squeezed his hands. "I-I care about you too. I enjoy spending time with you." She hesitated and drew in a breath. "But yes, the trip to Africa is definite and arrangements have been made. I won't be gone forever, but it's something I truly feel called to do." Her eyes glistened with unshed tears, and she nibbled her bottom lip as though trying not to cry.

No longer able to hold back, Shaun leaned in and gently placed his lips on hers. He only permitted himself a quick kiss, to affirm his feelings for her. Then he braced himself for her reaction. Would she think him too bold—perhaps slap his face?

To his delight and relief, she lowered her eyes and smiled. A somewhat sad smile, but he felt it acknowledged that Sadie wasn't offended nor thought him too forward.

Shaun spoke above a whisper. "I know it's selfish of me wanting you to stay here in Riverview. If being a missionary is your calling, then I'm sure you want to follow that. But I want to spend every minute possible with you before you leave, and please promise you'll write to me?" A lump had formed in his throat—something that didn't happen to Shaun O'Leary. He was a man who kept his emotions under control. When he did have sorrow or remorse, he concealed it. That's how he had been after losing Grace.

What was happening to him now? Apparently, Sadie Perkins had shown him otherwise. Where his feelings were concerned, he was much more transparent than he'd thought.

~ ~ ~ ~

The next morning at Miss Callie's table after breakfast, Shaun couldn't focus. Once the breakfast dishes had been cleared away, the landlady wiped the table to a sparkling shine, then told Shaun he was welcome to use the table until supper time.

But as he stared at the papers spread before him, he may as well have been trying to read Chinese. His mind wasn't cooperating, and he needed to make a decision about the house and property. Not to mention the fact his father was awaiting a reply to the telegram he'd sent. He could only imagine George O'Leary's scowl as he complained to Shaun's mother about the lack of information he'd received.

When had his life become so complicated? He'd thought being given the hotel project to handle would be wonderful. If things had gone as planned, perhaps it would have been. How was Shaun to know he'd fall in love with a woman in Riverview? A woman with emotional ties to the house he needed to demolish.

There had been no word from Harry Davis, so he assumed the man was still ill or either didn't want to carry through with the project. He blew out a frustrated breath and rubbed his forehead, then allowed his thoughts to drift back to the previous evening.

The carriage ride with Sadie had been perfect. Seated beside her as their driver took them on a delightful ride along tree-lined streets, Shaun was amazed at the contented feeling he had. A few times he'd gotten a whiff of her lavender scent, and the sound of her light laughter was a melody to his ears. And soul. But the best part of the evening was the sweet kiss. Although it had only been a brief one, Sadie's smile afterward melted his heart.

Now the papers spread before Shaun mocked him. What was he doing? Daydreaming about a woman he'd grown to love rather than working on the important project he'd been given. Shaun huffed out another frustrated sigh, then stuffed the papers into his satchel. After placing the satchel in his room, he decided to head outdoors. Perhaps if he went to the property on Willow Lane and spent some time there, he'd reach a decision regarding the next steps he should take. After all, remaining seated at Miss Callie's table had gotten him nowhere that morning.

"Will you be here for the evening meal, Mr. O'Leary?" Miss Callie was polishing furniture in the parlor as Shaun passed the room to leave.

"Yes, ma'am. I look forward to another delicious meal you've prepared." He noted the pleased look in her eyes.

The temperature was pleasant, and the sun peeked through clouds overhead. He knew from living at the coast his entire life that storms could come up in a hurry, but today the weather wouldn't include storms, so he could take his time. As Shaun headed toward Willow Lane, he tried not to think about how much he would miss Sadie.

No one strolled on the street other than Shaun, although voices drifted from a nearby street. The laughter of children playing, and the bark of a dog brought an unexpected smile to his face. If he ever had children, he would get them a dog.

Children. That didn't seem likely in his future—at least not anytime soon. He remembered Sadie's comment about how much she loved children. That's why she felt called to do her mission work helping orphans. Why did all of his thoughts take him back to Sadie?

He arrived at the property, now seeing the house from a different viewpoint than he had previously. Yes, it was a lovely house. But now it seemed even lovelier, because it held special meaning for Sadie.

Focus, O'Leary. The mental chiding reminded him why he was standing on the property. Shaun needed to see if there was any possibility of having the hotel constructed while leaving the house standing. He avoided muddy spots, still visible from recent rains the town had experienced.

Moseying from the left end of the property, he tried to visualize where the hotel might be erected beside the house. Perhaps if the architect altered the plans, it might work. Of course, having additional plans drawn up would incur yet another expense, and George O'Leary would frown on that.

He paused and gazed up at several trees on the property.

Shaun planned to leave as many as possible when the construction began. The stately oaks added so much to the lay of the land.

As the sun went behind clouds, the sky grew surprisingly darker. He hoped rain wouldn't follow, and the sun would make another appearance. A refreshing breeze blew and seemed to gather strength. The tree branches rustled overhead, as though a giant hand shook the oaks.

Then—he heard it. A cracking sound, followed by a loud snap. Before Shaun could take a step, an intense pain hit him. Everything went black.

~ ~ ~ ~

Glancing out the library window, Sadie saw the sky darkening. It appeared ominous—she much preferred the bright sunshine. No doubt rain was headed their way. Hopefully it would be gone before she pedaled home on her bicycle. Since hours remained before her workday ended, she pushed aside thoughts concerning inclement weather.

Sadie busied herself organizing the shelves and assisting patrons searching for books on particular topics. It was difficult to keep her mind from drifting back to the previous evening. The lovely carriage ride and meal with Shaun seemed almost magical now. He had declared his feelings, so she had no doubt that Shaun O'Leary cared deeply for her. The fact that she cared deeply for him also only added to the jumbled emotions within her.

With her mission trip approaching, she needed to focus solely on preparations for her journey. Yet her thoughts— and her heart—kept returning to the handsome man from Savannah. *Why, Lord? Why is someone coming into my life at this point, just as I'm preparing to sail to another country and work for You?* She released a frustrated sigh.

"Sadie, are feeling unwell?" Polly White stood beside her, a curious expression on her face. "Do you have a headache? If so, please feel free to step into our break room and rest a bit. We're not so busy that I cannot handle things myself." The librarian gazed at her with her head tilted.

Why had she become so caught up in her private musings that her boss even noticed an odd expression on her face? She needed to concentrate on the task at hand.

Forcing a smile, Sadie thanked the older woman. "That's kind. But I'm fine. I guess my thoughts drifted to all I must accomplish before leaving for Africa."

Polly patted her arm and smiled. "You have a lot on your shoulders these days. But if you do need a break, please remember it's fine with me. You've been a faithful, hardworking employee here at the library, and you'll be sorely missed."

At that moment a woman with several children approached the librarian with a question, so Polly turned to assist them. Sadie returned to her tasks, attempting to keep her mind on her job and a pleasant expression on her face.

A few minutes later Miss Callie rushed into the library, flushed and out of breath. Her eyes darted around. When she spotted Polly White, Miss Callie hurried to her and whispered something to her.

Although concerned and curious, Sadie continued with her work and didn't move closer to the women. The librarian would share if it was a bit of gossip.

At the same moment, both women stared directly at Sadie, and Polly gestured for her to join them.

Sadie couldn't imagine what was going on, but did as her boss requested. Worry etched both their features. Something was wrong.

"Sadie, Miss Callie just learned some news and was sure you'd want to know." Before Polly could say more, Sadie's heart raced. Had something happened to her father? Her breath caught and she opened her mouth to inquire, but Miss Callie spoke up.

"A man was in an accident on Willow Lane, and he's

with Doc Wilson at the moment. Hopefully he will be okay, but he's asking for you." A mixture of curiosity and concern were obvious in Miss Callie's eyes. She reached out and patted Sadie's arm. "Mrs. White has assured me it's fine for you to leave your job at the moment, and I'll be happy to walk with you to Doc Wilson's place."

"Who is it?" Sadie knew the answer, but had to make sure.

"Mr. O'Leary. A heavy branch from a large oak tree fell on him and it knocked him out, the poor man. As you might know, he's one of my boarders and is such a nice, polite man." Miss Callie shook her head and her face held remorse. "If you'll fetch whatever you have here, then I'll walk with you to see him."

Sadie numbly turned to retrieve her reticule underneath the front counter. She paused and looked at her boss. "Are you certain you don't mind my leaving now, Mrs. White? I will return as soon as possible." Sadie was already at the door when Polly answered.

"It is fine, and you don't need to return at all this afternoon. In fact, I'd feel much better if you went home after you check on Mr. O'Leary. You still have much to do in preparation for Africa, and I can manage fine the remainder of the day." She offered a reassuring smile to Sadie, then added. "And I'll be praying for Mr. O'Leary. I don't know him well, but he does seem like a nice man."

After nodding her thanks, Sadie hurried out the door with Miss Callie on her heels. The two women strode in silence to the next street, where Doc Wilson's home and his office were located.

Still somewhat numb, Sadie prayed. *Dear Lord, please help Shaun be okay. I don't know the details of what happened, but please help him heal from this accident.*

As the women turned into the yard of the Wilson home, Miss Callie touched Sadie's arm. "I feel sure the doctor has been taking good care of him. After I see you inside, I'll return to my boarding house. That is, unless you need me." Kindness exuded from Miss Callie's eyes.

"Thank you so much. There's no need for you to stay, as you have work to do. But I'm puzzled how you learned about the accident? Did you see it happen?" She didn't want to sound disrespectful in questioning the older woman, but was still trying to process the news.

They reached the small front porch of the doctor's house. Miss Callie shook her head. "No, I didn't witness it happening. It seems that a man who resides on Willow Lane was out searching for his dog, and he saw Mr. O'Leary lying on the ground, underneath a tall oak tree. A large, heavy branch lay on him, so it was obvious right away what happened." She clicked her tongue. "The poor man. That must've been so painful, and the branch hit him with enough force to knock him out cold." Miss Callie shuddered.

Tears formed in Sadie's eyes, but she kept them at bay. Breaking down would not help matters at all.

Miss Callie continued her explanation. "So the man ran and fetched a neighbor, and they carried Mr. O'Leary to Doc Wilson, who was in his office at the time, thank the Lord. Doc Wilson had seen Mr. O'Leary entering my boardinghouse, so rightfully assumed he was one of my boarders. The doctor sent his wife to fetch me, so I could identify Mr. O'Leary, who was beginning to rouse when I arrived." She paused to catch her breath. "But I have to say, seeing him with those injuries and knowing he'd been knocked out almost caused me to cry. That man did not deserve that, but I'm thankful he should be okay."

Sadie listened, but was eager to see Shaun for herself. Yet she also dreaded seeing him in such pain. Miss Callie had mentioned injuries, so Sadie braced herself while Miss Callie knocked at the door.

The doctor called for them to enter, Sadie stepped inside. Miss Callie gave her a gentle prod from close behind, no doubt for moral support.

The doctor greeted them, thanked Miss Callie for her assistance, and then spoke directly to Sadie. As the doctor talked to Sadie, Miss Callie slipped out the door.

"Thank you for coming as Mr. O'Leary has been asking for you." An unmistakable hint of amusement flashed through the doctor's eyes, and he rubbed his chin.

"Will he be okay?" Sadie attempted to keep her voice steady. She was more than a little relieved when the physician assured her Shaun would recover completely, but would have some bruises and pain for a while.

"He was fortunate, because if the branch had hit a few more inches over, it likely would've put out an eye. Although it fell hard enough to render him unconscious, I have no doubt he will make a complete recovery. He really needs to rest and refrain from any strenuous activity for at least a week. Possibly longer."

When the doctor led Sadie into the next room to see Shaun, she could no longer hold back her tears. Seeing him on the cot, head bandaged and bloodstains on his clothing, she wanted to kneel beside him and kiss his cheek. She didn't, of course, but the urge was there nonetheless.

She crouched down next to the cot. Then Shaun sleepily opened his eyes, then winced.

"S-Sadie...you came to see m-me—" Each word seemed to require effort. He raised an arm as if to reach his head.

"Oh Shaun, I'm so sorry you were injured, but Doc Wilson says you'll be fine. What can I do for you?" She had already swiped at her tears and hoped he didn't notice them.

A smile spread slowly across his face. "Nothing, but thanks...my head h-hurts so bad—" His voice trailed off in pain, and Sadie cast a worried look at the doctor.

"That's to be expected, I'm sorry to say. I've given him some pain medicine, and he can rest here until he's strong enough to be driven by carriage back to Miss Callie's—most likely later today. At the moment, he only needs rest, and I think he will feel better now that he's seen you." Doc Wilson grinned, sending a quick wink in Sadie's direction.

Her face warmed into a blush.

After assuring Shaun she would check on him again at Miss Callie's, Sadie returned to the main room of the house, with the doctor following closely behind.

"Please let me know if there's anything at all I can do for him. Mrs. White insisted I not return to the library this afternoon, so I'll be at home. Thank you for taking good care of him." Sadie smiled at the kind doctor she'd known for many years, then left his office with her reticule still clasped in her hands.

As she walked toward her home, she stopped. *Her bicycle!* It was still parked at the library, so she needed to return there after all. Sadie turned in the other direction and headed to the Riverview Library. After arriving, she hurried inside to check on Polly White.

The librarian assured her things were fine, and remained insistent that Sadie go home.

As Sadie pedaled away from the library, she thought about the accident, and decided to ride to Willow Lane. She wanted to see where the tree branch had fallen on Shaun.

When she reached the front yard of the house, she stopped and set the kickstand on her bicycle. Stepping around mud, she ventured around the house to a side yard area. There she saw it. An enormous branch lying on the ground—apparently weakened from the recent rain, or perhaps it had been struck by lightning. Whatever had caused it to detach, the branch had crashed down at the exact moment Shaun was underneath the tree.

A shudder raced up her spine. Normally she enjoyed seeing the majestic oak trees in the area, but at the moment this particular one didn't appear beautiful to Sadie. She needed to return home. Walking around the yard of her dream house wouldn't help Shaun, and besides, she had plenty to do at home.

After seeing the size of the culprit branch, Shaun was

blessed he hadn't been injured even worse. The Lord protected him, she knew without a doubt. Sadie also knew the Lord would show her exactly what to do about her future.

Chapter Nine

That evening Sadie was tired—more than tired, she was exhausted. Her recent jumble of emotions due to feelings for Shaun and preparing for overseas mission work resulted in Sadie feeling drained. After learning about Shaun's injury and seeing him so badly hurt, Sadie had no energy at all.

At least she was almost finished with the dishes, then she could read her Bible and prepare for bed. During the evening meal, she'd informed her father about the events of her day. He expressed great concern over Shaun and told Sadie he'd pray for the man. Sadie knew he was sincere, because her papa was a godly man and kept his word.

The next day, Sadie finished her morning ablutions, ate a piece of bread with jam, then climbed onto her bicycle to ride to the boardinghouse. Silently praying, her heart hammered in apprehension.

What if Shaun had been injured more than Doc Wilson realized? Sadie shoved the worry from her mind. The town's beloved physician was wise, and Sadie couldn't think of a single time he had made a diagnosis and been proven wrong.

Where was her faith? She mentally chided herself as she parked her bicycle outside Miss Callie's boardinghouse. Walking up the sidewalk to the front porch, Sadie noticed all the welcoming touches the woman had made. Flowers lined the walkway and pots of blooms on the porch greeted anyone who stopped by—whether a boarder or a guest.

Remnant aromas from breakfast lingered in the air, and Sadie remembered that she'd heard Miss Callie was an excellent cook. At least while Shaun rented a room in her house, he would be eating well. That thought gave Sadie a bit of comfort.

After knocking at the door, she was welcomed inside by Miss Callie, who told her in a soft voice that Shaun was resting. "The doctor arranged for a carriage to bring him here last night. And don't you worry, I'm checking on him every little bit. As soon as he's able to eat, I'll fix him something—most likely soup or something not too heavy."

Smiling in appreciation, Sadie reached out and patted the woman's arm. "Thank you. You've been most kind, and I'm sure once Shaun recovers he will be grateful for your help." She paused, feeling awkward. After all, she and Shaun were not related and no one in Riverview knew of her feelings for the man. Did they? Was she that easy to read? Sadie shoved that thought from her mind.

"Is there anything I can do to help you? I'm not supposed to work at the library today, so if you need me to go on an errand or do anything to help you, I'd be happy to do so." Sadie hoped the older woman realized her sincerity.

Apparently, she did, because she gave Sadie a warm smile and touched her shoulder. "No thank you. But you're so kind to offer. I'm a tough old bird and keep going even when something unexpected happens." She chuckled before becoming serious.

"I do want to ask about your upcoming trip. Are you still planning to leave for Africa soon?" Miss Callie's voice held a hint of uncertainty.

"That is my plan, unless the Lord shows me otherwise." Sadie smiled, hoping to appear confident. Although at the moment she felt anything but confident. It was probably due to being so tired.

Miss Callie looked down a moment, then brought her gaze back up to meet Sadie's. Clearing her throat, she spoke in a soft but serious tone. "Well, I think it's wonderful that you have that desire. But you must be absolutely certain it's the Lord's will before you set foot onto the ship that will take you across the ocean. And I'll pray for you." Her countenance changed. "Now, while you're here, step into my kitchen and I'll wrap up some cookies I've baked this morning. You can take some home for you and your father to enjoy."

Minutes later, Sadie left Miss Callie's boardinghouse with a wrapped package of oatmeal raisin cookies. She placed them in the wicker basket of her bicycle, then pedaled home. Miss Callie's words echoed in her mind with every turn of the pedal. *Be absolutely certain it's the Lord's will.*

Was Sadie certain her mission trip was the Lord's will? New doubts nudged her, and she had to swerve to miss a dog that was about to cross her path. She needed to pay attention as she rode her bicycle, or she'd end up having an accident herself.

She pushed away thoughts of Miss Callie's well-meaning comment and thought about Shaun. Although disappointed she hadn't been able to see him for herself, she knew he was being well-cared for. Perhaps Miss Callie had been a nurse at one time, because the woman seemed at ease tending to an injured tenant in addition to running her boarding house.

Lucy called out to her as Sadie steered her bicycle into her yard.

With flushed cheeks her widowed friend ran up to her. "I heard about poor Shaun, and I'm so very sorry. Is he going to be okay?" She clasped one hand to her bosom and the other clutched a small bouquet of flowers.

"Yes, he should be fine. Let me park my bicycle and we can go inside. I'll tell you all about it." Hastily putting her bicycle into Papa's small storage shed, Sadie then led Lucy into the Perkins' kitchen.

"I was returning from Miss Callie's just now. She's looking after Shaun as he recovers from his injury. Isn't that wonderful?" She went on to give details of what Doc Wilson had told her.

Lucy shuddered. "Oh my, thank the good Lord that the branch didn't put out his eye."

Sadie nodded, then Lucy giggled. "Here, I'm still holding these, and you need to put them in a vase of water. Mother grew them in her little garden, and after we heard about Shaun we both knew you'd be upset. It's a little something to cheer you up." Lucy thrust the bouquet toward Sadie. A cluster of colorful zinnias and yellow marigolds tied together with a thin green ribbon made a cheerful nosegay.

Unexpected tears filled Sadie's eyes. "Thank you—these are beautiful. Please tell your sweet mother I said thank you also." Sadie sniffed, hoping the tears would stop. *Why had she suddenly began crying again? Was it because of her fatigue, or from feeling so emotional?*

Lucy noticed the tears right away and leaned over to bestow a quick hug. "Are you still upset about Shaun's accident? You said Doc Wilson assured you he'll be fine, and Doc Wilson is never mistaken." A concerned frown shadowed Lucy's face.

Sadie shook her head, embarrassed in front of her best friend. "No, I'm sure he'll be fine, as you said. You're right about Doc Wilson too—he's always correct. It's just—" Her voice trailed off and she plopped into a kitchen chair, still clasping the bouquet of flowers.

"It's just everything. I'm so tired, and I'm nervous about sailing to Africa. Although I believe that's what I'm supposed to do, I will admit I'm anxious about the journey. Not to mention leaving Papa, and you, and everyone in Riverview." A deep sigh escaped her mouth.

Lucy gave her a bittersweet smile and completed Sadie's thoughts. "And Shaun? You're sad about leaving him too, aren't you? I'm your best friend and know you well, so I can see it in your eyes. You care about him, and you're wondering if you're doing the right thing in leaving."

Silence hung in the air. The ticking of the kitchen clock was the only sound. Then Sadie looked directly at Lucy and nodded.

"Yes, you're right." She went on to share Miss Callie's earlier comments, about being certain it was the Lord's will. "After I left Miss Callie's house, more doubts came into my mind. I suppose this means I need to pray a lot more. I sure can't sail across the ocean if I'm not completely certain I'm doing the right thing." Frustrated, Sadie leaped up from the kitchen table. Opening a cabinet, she lifted out a small vase to fill with water for the flowers. After placing water and the blooms in the vase, she set it on the kitchen table and smiled.

"These do cheer me up, so thank you." Yes, the vase of colorful spring blooms did indeed bring a touch of cheer to the room, and to Sadie's mood. But she must spend more time in prayer and searching her Bible. She had to be certain before she set foot on the ship.

~ ~ ~ ~

Shaun didn't think his head had ever hurt so badly. Not even after nights in Riley's Tavern in Savannah, some years back. But this pain was temporary and should make him appreciate feeling better once he recovered.

The events of the past twenty-four hours were a hazy blur, but certain things remained clear. Sadie visited him in Doc Wilson's office, and he remembered being transported by a carriage from the doctor's house to Miss Callie's boardinghouse. Also, Miss Callie had been an angel of mercy to him, checking on him and bringing him a bowl of soup. She also kept an eye on his head wound, checking under the bandage and supplying more ice when needed. Yes, he was a lucky man indeed.

Gradually he remembered why he'd been on the property, and he blew out a frustrated sigh. He had gone to Willow Lane in hopes of determining a different placement of the hotel, so the house could remain standing. That's what he'd been doing when he heard the snap of the large, heavy branch. The memory made him wince. Best not to think about that at the moment.

Regarding his job, Shaun had no other choice. As soon as he was able, he'd take a train to Savannah and talk face-to-face with his father. Even if George O'Leary scoffed, Shaun would plead the case of Sadie and the house.

Sadie. How he longed to see her again. Miss Callie told him that Sadie stopped by to check on him that morning, but he'd been resting. He absolutely had to recover soon so he could spend time with her before she left for Africa. That thought made his heart race and his head throbbed even more. The last thing he wanted was for her to leave, but the choice was not his to make.

A soft tapping at the door interrupted his thoughts. Doc Wilson poked his gray head around the door. "May I come in?"

"Of course. I owe you a big thank you, in addition to a payment." Shaun attempted to chuckle, but every movement or sound required effort, which was still difficult in his weakened, hurting condition.

"You don't worry about payin' me just yet. You concentrate on healing and gettin' back to normal. I don't know if you realize it yet, but you got hit by a mighty large, thick branch. Your injuries could've been much worse." The physician stroked his clean-shaven chin, his eyes studying Shaun.

Shaun slowly nodded, trying not to make the pain in his head worse. "Yes, I was very lucky."

To Shaun's surprise the doctor frowned and shook his head. "No son, 'twern't luck at all. The good Lord was watchin' over you and protecting you."

Apparently, the physician could read Shaun's face and figured out he wasn't a believer. For the next half-hour, the doctor sat by Shaun's bedside, telling him about Jesus Christ dying on a cross for everyone's sins. His delivery was no-nonsense and he got straight to the point, explaining salvation in a way that made Shaun's heart burdened. When the older man finished speaking, silence hung in the air.

When Shaun decided to speak, his voice trembled, and his eyes filled with moisture. He knew what he needed to do.

After praying with the doctor, Shaun had no doubt he was a changed man. After the men said good-bye a little later, Shaun wanted to leap from his bed, but knew he couldn't. Not yet. But he could talk to Sadie and was eager to do so. He imagined the look on her face when he shared his salvation with her. But before he could think of how he would tell her, Shaun drifted into a deep slumber, and didn't rouse until Miss Callie brought supper into his room.

~ ~ ~ ~

Why was the time fleeting? Sadie asked herself while she worked at the library the following day. Shoving memories of the past few days from her mind, she instead thought about Lucy and Matthew. Today he was to arrive in Riverview, and Lucy was beyond excited. How Sadie hoped and prayed a lasting relationship would develop for them, because she'd never seen Lucy this happy.

"A message was just delivered for you." Polly White paused, looking puzzled. "One of the boarders at Miss Callie's house left this note, and then he left. I hope nothing is wrong." The librarian eyed the note in her hand as though wanting to tear it open herself, but refrained from doing so.

"Thank you." Sadie took the note and opened it with trembling hands. Curiosity mingled with fear coursed through her. She read the brief message, then re-read it. A note from Miss Callie informed her that all was well, but Shaun had requested to see her on her lunch break.

Her boss hovered close by, and the poor woman was about to burst with curiosity. Sadie explained the note's contents.

"By all means, dear. You make certain to go over to the boardinghouse to check on Mr. O'Leary. And I don't mind a bit if you take extra time. I'm just thankful he's going to be okay, after that terrible injury."

Thanking the librarian, Sadie returned to her tasks, finding it almost impossible to focus on what she was doing. What could Shaun want to tell her? Surely his health hadn't taken a turn for the worse, because Miss Callie had written that all was well. The woman wouldn't have added that statement if there was something wrong.

She mulled the note over in her mind and told herself he only wanted to reassure her he was going to be well. Perhaps he'd received news about the hotel construction. Maybe the entire project had been cancelled. No, that would be too good to be true.

When her lunchtime arrived, Polly White insisted she leave to visit Shaun. Sadie didn't argue, but thanked her boss and made a hasty exit.

Pedaling her bicycle as quickly as possible, Sadie felt moisture forming on her neck. Oh dear, why hadn't she pinned her air up on her head? She didn't want to look like a farmhand coming in from the field when she saw Shaun, but with the heat and her windblown hair, she was sure to be a mess.

Miss Callie greeted her right away at the door and ushered her to Shaun's room. Embarrassed, Sadie hovered near the door.

Shaun's face lit up when he saw her. He was looking a little better, though still bearing bandages. "Thank you for coming to see me. I hope this doesn't create a problem at the library with your work." His brow furrowed.

With a chuckle, Sadie explained how concerned Mrs. White had been. "She's been worried about you, and insisted I take a longer lunch break to come and see you. You've made quite an impression on her." Sadie giggled, thinking of how he'd certainly made an impression on her, too.

"I don't want to take up much of your time, but wanted to share that Doc Wilson was here this morning to check on me. He gave me a good report on my recovery, but the best news was what the man did for my soul." Tears formed in Shaun's eyes, and he blinked them away.

Was he feeling the effects of some pain medication? Perhaps he had a fever and was talking out of his head. She inched closer to his bedside.

Shaun winced after shifting to face her.

"Sadie, the doctor talked with me about Jesus. He explained everything as I've never heard it before. I have finally realized that I cannot run from the Lord—I need Him too much." He paused as though gathering his strength and thoughts, then continued. "He prayed with me, and I-I asked the Lord into my heart. And into my life." He paused again, then gazed into Sadie's eyes. "I'm far from perfect, and always will be. But I have a peace now, Sadie. A peace I'd never felt before. And I wanted to tell you." He sniffed and swiped at his eyes.

Tears streamed down her face and she leaned closer to him. She reached down with a trembling hand and brushed a tear from his cheek. "That is the most wonderful news I've ever heard. Thank you for telling me." If she continued to speak, she'd end up sobbing—from joy and relief. Instead, Sadie simply smiled at the man she loved with all her heart. The man she wasn't sure if she could ever leave.

~ ~ ~ ~

The following week Sadie began setting out items to take with her to Africa. Why was her heart so heavy? She'd always thought when she reached this point, she would be so excited about fulfilling her dream of mission work that her steps would be light.

Her thoughts traveled back to the previous Saturday when she and Papa had joined Lucy's family for dinner. The evening was a delightful time of eating and visiting with Lucy and Matthew. But for Sadie, the best part of the evening was observing Lucy's happiness every time she looked at Matthew.

As happy as she was for her friend, Sadie would never experience that. After all, she was to remain single and do mission work. Wasn't she? Plagued with doubts and second thoughts, she prayed even more and searched her Bible for guidance. The verses reminded her that the Lord would show her what to do. At the moment, things still appeared pointed at Africa.

"Sadie girl, Pastor Lucas and his wife want to have a little going-away party for you before you sail out." Her father's words seemed to require effort, and Sadie knew he was struggling to release his only daughter to mission work.

"Oh, that's so kind of them. But please tell them I said no. I don't mean to sound ungrateful, but if I gather with our Riverview friends, it'll make my leaving that much harder." Sadie's eyes filled with tears. Her father nodded, apparently understanding his daughter was sincere.

"Okay. I'll give them the message. I don't blame you a bit, because I think celebratin' should be saved for when you return home." He shuffled to the living room, his steps tired and heavy.

Tired and heavy seemed to describe Sadie's heart these days. But she still had much to do, so she forced herself to keep moving. Each time she glanced at the calendar on the shelf in the living room, she felt a sense of dread. The days were indeed passing too quickly.

She was eager to see Shaun again, thankful that he'd recovered from his injuries—at least for the most part—he'd taken a train to Savannah. Before leaving, however, he assured Sadie he'd return to Riverview and spend time with her before she left for Africa.

"Papa, I'm going out for a little walk. I think some fresh air will be good, and then I'll return to my packing." After assuring Papa she'd be back before dark, Sadie left the cozy cottage. Moses and Levi gazed lazily up at her as she stepped off the porch, and Sadie was thankful she didn't have to worry about her cats following her. Both felines would be waiting on her when she returned home shortly.

Without giving it much thought, she felt drawn to Willow Lane and to her dream house. She remained on the sidewalk, gazing at the house. Memories of walks with her mother filled her mind, along with more recent dreams of returning from mission work to open a home for children who needed loving care.

Fighting the tears that threatened to cascade down her face, Sadie drew in a deep breath. Birds were singing their evening concert, with crickets chirping in the background. The fragrance of wild honeysuckle reached her nostrils, and a light breeze stirred, making the air smell fresher. All the familiar sounds and scents of her hometown—that she would miss terribly.

Dusk was fast approaching, so Sadie took one more longing look at the house, then turned to walk home. As her steps brought her closer to her cottage, Sadie thought about the country she'd be sailing to—the country that would be her home for perhaps a year. From everything she'd read and heard, Africa would be vastly different from her coastal Georgia town. Surely she could adjust in time with the Lord's help. She only needed to remain focused on helping the orphans in her care and teaching them about Jesus.

I will instruct thee and teach thee in the way which thou shalt go. The familiar verse went through Sadie's mind, and she knew beyond any doubt, the words were true. The Lord would show her clearly—if she would only trust and follow His leading. So why was her heart so heavy?

~ ~ ~ ~

The train rolled along at a fairly good speed, but Shaun wanted it to go even faster. He was eager to be in Riverview and see Sadie again. He'd missed her so much and wanted to be with her every minute possible before she left.

His meeting with his father had gone okay, but not as well as Shaun had expected. George O'Leary hadn't scoffed at Shaun's explanation of the house on Willow Lane and what it meant to Sadie. Rather, he'd looked at his son with pity, making Shaun wish his father had scoffed at him.

His father's words replayed in his mind as the train took Shaun closer to Riverview. "So you've developed an interest in a woman in Riverview, eh? Tell me about her son. She must be something special to have captured your heart."

Shaun tried to keep his voice casual and give a quick description of Sadie, assuring his father that she was a fine young lady. He was relieved when his father nodded his approval, but George's nod quickly turned to a worried frown as he reminded Shaun of his mother's wishes.

"You know your mother is still counting on you courting one of Savannah's debutantes. Ever since poor Grace departed this world, may she rest in peace, and left you a widower, your mother has had high aspirations for you."

At those words Shaun had bristled—not toward his father, but at the thought that Colleen O'Leary was intent on planning her son's future.

Shaun brought their conversation back to the business details of the hotel project. To Shaun's pleasant surprise, his father was willing to have the architect walk around the property again to see if the plans could be altered to accommodate the house and leave it intact.

"It doesn't seem likely, Shaun, but given that you care so much for this Sadie woman, I'm willing to have the architect attempt it."

Shaun had never felt as close to his father as he did during that talk. Finally, George O'Leary seemed to care about what his son wanted. Of course, perhaps the fact that Shaun could've been injured even worse in the tree branch mishap helped soften the older man's feelings. Whatever the reason, Shaun's heart was lighter and happier than he could remember feeling as he'd left Savannah for Riverview.

Until he allowed himself to think about the woman he loved leaving for Africa. Was that truly what Sadie was supposed to do? Shaun had been praying for her, now that he had a relationship with the Lord. Although he was tempted to pray that she'd stay in Riverview, that would be selfish, so his prayer was that Sadie would do the Lord's will.

But how his heart ached to think of her leaving for a place so far away. The porter hollered out and snapped Shaun from his thoughts. "Riverview, next stop!" The man's bellowing voice startled an older man who'd been napping across from Shaun.

Shaun could hardly wait to be with Sadie, but he should contact the architect right away. No, he would listen to his heart. He would visit with Sadie and let her know what he and his father were trying to do. It would help ease her mind if she knew her dream house might not be torn down after all.

After depositing his bags at Miss Callie's boardinghouse and assuring her that he was doing much better, Shaun hurried to Sadie's cottage, noticing with amusement her beloved cats sitting in a window. Sadie would miss Moses and Levi while she was away.

When she answered the door, her face lit up, causing Shaun's heart to do flips. It was all he could do not to grab her in a hug and plant a kiss on those sweet lips.

Instead, he grinned at her. "Do I look a little better now that I'm not wearing a bandage across my head?" He chuckled and was glad to see her giggling.

"How did your trip back home to Savannah go? I'm sure your family was happy to see you." Shaun didn't miss the look of worry in her eyes. She must be wondering about the hotel project.

With a nod he replied. "It was nice to see my family again—and our housekeeper Maude. She's like family to me, because she always acts happier to see me than the others." He laughed, then went on to tell Sadie about his meeting with his father. "I'm relieved my father is agreeable to seeing if the architect can draw up additional plans for the hotel. Plans that would allow the house—your dream house—to remain standing." He paused to gauge her reaction, but was unprepared for what followed.

Tears flowed down her cheeks. She brought a hand up to her mouth and sniffled. "Oh Shaun, I can't believe you're going to this trouble for me." The tears continued to flow.

Unable to stand it any longer, Shaun embraced her in a warm hug. "I love you, and there's nothing I wouldn't do for you. Please believe me." He continued holding her until her crying subsided. Then he stepped back to gaze down at her. Even with a tear-streaked face, Sadie was beautiful.

She looked up at him with green eyes made brighter from the tears, under full, dark lashes. A smile played on her lips, and she giggled. "I must look a sight."

"Yes, you're a beautiful sight, Sadie Perkins." After a few moments of silence, Shaun cleared his throat. "I don't want to dampen the conversation, but my father did let me know there's a possibility the architect won't be able to draw up new plans to accommodate the house. But we're certainly going to try." He hoped his last statement would be enough to offer Sadie hope about the situation. She didn't need to be fretting about that house being torn down while preparing to leave for her mission work.

"I understand." She whispered, the chestnut hair around her face giving her the appearance of an innocent child.

"Now, please tell me how you've been. Are you getting ready for your trip?" Shaun tried to keep his voice upbeat but a sense of dread colored his tone.

Sadie shrugged. "I've been okay, thank you for asking. And yes, I'm getting my trunk packed for my journey. This is all so new to me since I've never even sailed on a ship. Only the ferry when I went with my friend Lucy to visit St. Simon's Island." She cringed, making Shaun wonder what had happened.

"That return trip to the mainland was terrible, because I became quite ill." She shuddered but then laughed.

"Well, let's hope you won't be seasick on the ship, and you'll be so excited about the children whom you'll be helping in Africa. So maybe thinking of the reason for your voyage will help keep your mind off the ocean." Even though Shaun doubted that would be the case, he wanted to offer encouragement to her. After all, she was doing this to help others, not something frivolous for herself. He also admired Sadie's honesty and openness with him, because some women he'd known in the past would never have admitted to becoming seasick.

There were so many things about Sadie that he loved—but most of all, he loved her.

And he didn't want to let her go, but he must. But he planned on being there when she returned. Whenever that would be.

After leaving Sadie's home, Shaun headed to the boardinghouse. He needed to devise a plan to contact the architect and decided his best option would be to hire a carriage and ride over to the architect's office in nearby Darien.

To Shaun's great relief, as his carriage driver steered the horse into Darien, it didn't take long to locate a small building bearing the sign, *Anderson Architects*. He hoped Mr. Elmer Louis Anderson would be in his office. Shaun almost held his breath as he entered the small lobby of the building.

A middle-aged woman, possibly Mrs. Anderson, Shaun supposed, was seated at a desk. "Good afternoon, sir. May I help you?"

"Good afternoon, ma'am. I don't have an appointment, but wondered if Mr. Elmer Louis Anderson is in this afternoon? He's the architect for a hotel I'm overseeing in Riverview, and I needed to speak with him concerning something that's come up."

The woman's face lit up. "Ah, you must be Mr. O'Leary of Savannah. Yes, my husband was happy to draw up the plans for your hotel. And as a matter of fact, my husband is in today, so you're in luck."

Although the woman was welcoming, Shaun was eager to meet with the architect and see if his idea was indeed possible.

Forty-five minutes later, Shaun left the Anderson Architect building, with a mixture of hope and apprehension battling within him. Mr. Anderson was agreeable about doing his best to draw up a second set of hotel plans, and assured Shaun he'd make every attempt to meet the specifications for the hotel while allowing the house to remain standing on the property. But he had also added the possibility that Shaun's idea would not work.

"I'll do the best I can. You have my word." The architect extended a beefy hand to seal his word, and Shaun thanked him and left.

On the return ride from Darien to Riverview, Shaun replayed the meeting in his mind. Mr. Anderson would need time to complete this new assignment, and it would also involve the architect visiting the property at least two or three times. Not to mention the added expense, since Mr. Anderson would need to be paid again for a second set of plans.

But I have to try—for Sadie's sake. Shaun thought of the woman he loved and what she was trying to accomplish. Without a doubt, Sadie had to be the most selfless woman he'd ever met. And the fact she was beautiful was an added benefit to her list of admirable qualities.

Glancing at his watch, Shaun realized it was almost time for supper at the boardinghouse. He'd been so preoccupied with thoughts of the hotel plans that he hadn't eaten since breakfast, and now his stomach rumbled.

He paid and thanked the carriage driver, then hurried into Miss Callie's, where tempting aromas greeted him. The other boarders were just coming into the dining room and Miss Callie was setting out a platter of fried chicken, along with bowls of potatoes, peas, and corn.

She glanced up and winked at Shaun. "You got back just in time. I'd hate for you to miss this meal I've been cooking all afternoon." She placed a basket of her feather-light biscuits and a saucer of creamery butter on the table.

Shaun grinned in return. "I'd hate to miss this meal too. Thank you for cooking it for us." He and the others bowed their heads as the landlady offered up a blessing.

As he bit into a piece of the crispy fried chicken, Shaun couldn't help but think back to previous meals at Miss Callie's. Before he'd accepted the Lord into his life, Shaun would lower his head out of respect for Miss Callie, but he wouldn't actually pray. Now all that changed, and Shaun was more than happy to offer up a prayer of thanks for the meals—in addition to his many other blessings.

~ ~ ~ ~

Pastor Lucas stopped by the Perkins' cottage several times a week to check on Sadie and see if she had any questions he could answer. "Although I haven't been to Africa myself, I have friends who've been there, serving as missionaries. So I've learned a good bit from them. If you think of any more questions, please feel free to ask and I'll do my best to answer. And remember that Mrs. Lucas and I, along with all your church family, are praying for you." The pastor grinned. "We're mighty proud of you, Sadie."

Were Pastor Lucas's eyes tearing up? She hoped not because that would cause her crying to start up again, something she'd done too much in the past few weeks. It was a wonder her eyes weren't constantly puffy and red.

"Only a few more days, and you'll be taking the schooner from Riverview to board the ship at the Savannah port. Very exciting, but even more important, you'll be doing the Lord's work, so He will watch over you."

Sadie's pulse raced at his words. Could Pastor Lucas tell by looking at her face that she was extremely nervous about the voyage itself? But then, why shouldn't she be nervous? As she told Shaun recently, she'd never sailed on a ship in her life, and her ferry ride resulted in her becoming ill.

Pasting on a smile, Sadie thanked the pastor. "You and Mrs. Lucas have been wonderful. And the Riverview Church too—I couldn't be doing this without all the support and prayers." Although she tried to appear composed, she was certain the pastor saw right through her.

Before leaving, he patted Sadie's arm and gave her a reassuring smile, the way her father did. She thanked him again for stopping by.

After he left, Sadie prepared the evening meal for Papa and herself. Soon her father entered their cottage. She always had a sense of relief when Papa arrived home, knowing he'd put in a hard day at the mill.

"Mmm...smells tasty, Sadie girl." Horace stepped into the kitchen, washed his hands, and sat in his chair. "I shouldn't tell you this, but I am going to miss you while you're away. And your cooking too, of course." Her father chuckled, eyeing the platter of sliced beef and the bowl of green beans Sadie had placed before him.

Trying to keep her voice light, she said, "Before you know it, I'll be home from Africa and cooking for you again. And don't worry. While I'm gone some of the ladies here in Riverview are going to look after you—they've assured me. So most likely you'll be invited to quite a few meals, and be bringing home leftovers." At least that's what Sadie hoped.

As they ate, Sadie told her father about the pastor's visit that afternoon, and inquired about his day at the mill. How she'd miss these talks with her father each day. But she'd write letters to him, and hopefully would receive a few back.

After the meal, Sadie washed their dishes and stepped out of the kitchen when a knock sounded at the front door. *Most likely it's Lucy, coming to talk about Matthew.* She grinned as she thought of her widowed friend's excitement over having a beau.

To Sadie's surprise, Shaun stood at her door, looking so attractive a tingle ran through her. "Come in." Hoping her voice wasn't breathless, Sadie welcomed him into the living room where Papa sat reading his evening newspaper.

The two men shook hands and exchanged greetings.

"I sure am glad to see you're over that injury, son. When Sadie told me about that big tree branch fallin' on you, I was a mite worried myself, and commenced to prayin'."

"Thank you, sir. I appreciate the concern—and the prayers. From now on, I'll need to pay careful attention when I walk under those large trees." Shaun chuckled and winked at Sadie.

"Would you like to visit on the front porch? I can pour you some lemonade or water if you'd like." Sadie had already taken a step toward the kitchen.

Shaun assured her he was fine and visiting on the porch would be nice. "There was a breeze stirring on my walk from Miss Callie's, so it's pleasant out this evening."

After they settled into the wicker chairs on the porch, Shaun told Sadie about his meeting with the architect that day. "There are no guarantees, but I do want you to know

I'm trying hard to ensure the house you love remains standing. The architect, Mr. Anderson, is going to try his best to draw a set of additional plans to allow for the altered dimensions. I made certain to explain that we want the house to remain untouched, and somehow fit the hotel on the land next to it." Shaun paused and released a long breath. "I do have faith in Mr. Anderson, and I feel if it's possible, he will find a way."

Sadie felt her heart leap. Shaun was going to such trouble for her. She was touched and reached out to clasp his hand in hers. "I'm honored. Thank you so much for doing this, now that you know how much the house means to me." She was fearful if she said much more, she'd become overcome with emotion.

"Now, I want to hear about your plans. Is your departure date still the same?" He paused. When she didn't answer him right away, he added, "I don't want you to leave. But I know in your heart you're doing what you feel called to do by the Lord, so that's the most important thing. You've got to follow the Lord's leading. It's terribly selfish of me to admit this, but if it were up to me, I'd have you remain here. Forever. With me." He added the last comment in a lowered voice, looking almost sheepish.

Taken aback, Sadie's mind raced. What was he saying? He'd already declared that he loved her, but was he talking about a lasting relationship? Her face warmed in a blush.

"I hope you know how much I care about you, too. And you're right about feeling called by the Lord." She paused and moistened her lips. "But you mentioned remaining here, as in Riverview. You live in Savannah." Perhaps she'd misunderstood his meaning.

He offered a wry-sounding chuckle. "Yes, my home actually is in Savannah, but after being in Riverview so much recently, I've grown fond of your little town." He raised an eyebrow. "I think it would be a nice place to live all the time."

Her mind whirled. Was he only saying this in an attempt to change her mind about leaving? Surely not. He realized the importance of what she was taking on, including all the effort and financial contributions that went into her mission work plans.

"Yes, Riverview is a nice town, and I'm thankful it's my home. I'll miss it terribly while I'm away." She drew in a shaky breath. "And yes, to answer your question my departure date is still the same. Three more days."

Shaun sprang to his feet and made a sweeping bow to her. "Well then, Miss Perkins, for the next two days what would you like to do? Shaun O'Leary at your service."

Sadie didn't know whether to laugh or cry, and to her dismay she did a little of both.

With giggles and tears she gazed up at him. "I'm afraid you're going to make it more difficult for me to leave." Realizing he was still waiting for her answer, she shrugged. "It doesn't matter what we do—I'm thankful to spend time with you. But what about your job?" She didn't expect Shaun to put his obligations on hold—even for only two days—while he spent time with her.

He reached down and pulled Sadie to her feet. "My job is at a standstill for the moment. I can't do anything else until the architect determines if he can draw up new hotel plans as requested. Is there anything I can help you do to prepare for Africa?" The caring gaze in his eyes made her want to collapse into his arms right then.

Wishing she didn't sound so breathless, she shook her head. "No, thank you. I'm all packed, and Papa and Pastor Lucas will see me off from the Riverview dock. I'll take a schooner and sail to Savannah, where I'll board the ship. The details are all planned, so it's only a matter of my arriving on time."

"Since it will be dark soon, how would it be if we start out tomorrow about ten o'clock and I'll surprise you." A twinkle lit his eyes, sending curious tingles running through her.

Why did this man have to be so handsome? Not to mention attentive and kind to her.

Later that night as she prepared for bed, Sadie thought how ironic it was the way her life events were flowing. After being certain she was to remain single and would never again have a beau, she planned on being a missionary. Now the most handsome man she'd ever seen admitted he loved her and wanted to spend time with her.

Dear Lord, if I'm still supposed to serve as a missionary—as I feel I am—please give me a peace about it. If I am not supposed to leave, please show me clearly.

Before drifting off to sleep, Sadie's mind was filled with thoughts of Shaun O'Leary, wondering about the surprise he'd planned for the following day.

~ ~ ~ ~

Sadie couldn't remember when she'd enjoyed a day so much. Except for the tugging at her heartstrings, knowing she'd be leaving soon, the day was perfect.

Shaun surprised her with a delightful carriage ride and a picnic lunch prepared by Miss Callie. The early summer weather added to the enjoyment of the day. Birds chirped and butterflies gracefully landed on flowers.

Feeling carefree, Sadie wished the day could last forever. What a precious memory to treasure in her heart as she made her ocean voyage and then settled in a foreign land.

"Please promise you'll write to me, and we'll be together when you return from Africa. Will you promise me that?" Shaun's voice was tender as was his gaze, his face only inches from hers.

Her heart pounded so hard she thought it might burst out of her chest, and she hoped Shaun didn't hear it. She nodded, feeling unable to speak at the moment. There was no denying she loved this man. So why was she leaving him, and forfeiting a future with him?

She knew the answer. Feeling called to the mission field, Sadie must go. If Shaun loved her, which she believed he did, then he'd wait for her. It would be difficult for both of them, but they could resume a relationship when she returned. Perhaps her mission service wouldn't be for a full year. Surely the time would speed by.

Before any more thoughts could tumble through her mind, Shaun's lips were about to kiss her. She closed her eyes and drank in his nearness. The kiss was gentle and lasted longer than the first one. Sadie felt as though she was melting into his arms. Yes, this man must truly love her, and she loved him every bit as much.

When he finally drew back, he gazed at her. When had a man ever loved her this much? Never. She hadn't known it was possible to feel this way, and now she didn't want this moment—or this feeling—to end.

But it had to, because the day was marching on. Sadie needed to return home to prepare her father's meal. She looked up at Shaun and smiled, thanking him for the wonderful day.

He squeezed her hand. "I had a wonderful day too. Please remember what I've asked you to promise me. I will be waiting for you when you return, and I will love you forever."

Chapter Ten

"No. There must be another solution." Shaun rubbed the back of his neck. His temples throbbed. The architect had arrived by carriage at the boarding house the next morning, surprising Shaun to see him so soon.

The pleasant surprise turned to dismay and frustration. The architect had kindly but firmly informed Shaun that given the dimensions of the land, there was no possible way to build the hotel and leave the house standing.

"Trust me, I've analyzed this and spent the entire day yesterday on nothing else. I rode to the property on Willow Lane, measured, and attempted various possibilities. All to no avail, I'm sorry to say. You remember I mentioned to you at our last meeting that I couldn't guarantee your idea would work, although I hoped it would. But given the type of hotel you and your father plan to construct, the house has to be torn down. Which is certainly a pity, I must say. It's a lovely structure and seems such a waste to demolish a perfectly good house." Mr. Anderson gave Shaun a look of sympathy mixed with frustration.

Shaun released a deep sigh. "I understand. You tried

your best to accommodate my suggestion, but it simply didn't work. I thank you for making the effort and working on this as quickly as you have done. Your payment will be forthcoming within the week, if that is agreeable." He shook the architect's hand.

"Certainly. That is fine, and please keep my company in mind if you need an architect in your future projects. I wish you the best in your endeavors."

After Elmer Louis Anderson left the boardinghouse, Shaun remained seated at the dining room table for a few minutes. He was thankful Miss Callie didn't serve a noonday meal so she didn't need her dining room at the moment. Propping his elbows on the table, Shaun covered his face with his hands. *What could he do?* The question taunted him over and over in his mind.

"Mr. O'Leary? Are you feeling ill? Is your head hurting from your recent injury?" Miss Callie's concerned voice reached his ears, and Shaun jerked his head up and winced. He hadn't heard the boardinghouse owner step into the dining room.

Shaun smiled at her. "No, I'm okay. Thank you for asking. I'm just feeling frustrated over some business matters, that's all. Do you need your table now?" He was prepared to hop up.

The landlady grinned and patted his arm. "No, you stay here as long as you want." Then she winked and added. "Well, at least until six o'clock. That's when the evening meal is served, as you well know." With a chuckle she returned to her kitchen, humming along the way.

Sitting at the table wouldn't accomplish anything, so he headed to his room and took out his papers and notes. Spreading them on his bed, he scowled. There was only one thing Shaun could do now, and that was to go ahead with the hotel project as planned. The house would be torn down while Sadie was overseas, so she wouldn't witness the actual demolition process. When she returned from her mission work, she'd be so occupied with continuing her work that the house would no longer matter.

Who are you kidding, O'Leary? You saw the tears in her eyes when she explained why the house means so much to her.

Heading out of the boardinghouse a little later Shaun knew he had no choice. His father's company had purchased the land with the sole intent of having a hotel constructed, and that's what must be done. And that meant the house must be demolished. Since the previous construction company hadn't contacted Shaun or his father, then another company would have to be found. Plans would need to be underway soon for the demolition before the construction could begin. Shaun had much work ahead of him.

His steps led him to the property on Willow Lane. Shaun stood on the sidewalk in front of the house, staring as if another solution would magically appear. Of course he knew better—there was no other solution.

"Shaun?" The female voice reached his ears, sending joy and fear running through him at the same time. He turned and smiled.

"Sadie! Are you taking one more walk in Riverview before you leave tomorrow? I was planning to visit with you later today since I've been busy with work this morning." He saw the expectant look in her eyes, which only added to his nervousness about questions she was certain to ask.

"Yes, I thought I'd take another walk—especially since I'll be confined to a ship out on the Atlantic Ocean for a while." She released a deep, heavy sigh. Her green eyes lacked the sparkle he'd seen in the past.

He grabbed her hands and stared into her eyes. "Are you absolutely certain this is what you want to do? What you truly feel called to do?" Shaun hated the pleading tone in his voice, but in essence that's what he was doing. He was pleading with her. He loved this woman and didn't want her to leave.

It would be different if Sadie was only traveling to another city—or even another state. But across the sea to another country was breaking his heart. Just as he knew her heart would be broken when she learned about the house.

"I've done so much praying and searching my Bible, and still feel this is what I'm supposed to do. Please don't make it harder for me to leave tomorrow."

"I'm sorry. I just love you so much." He wanted to kiss her right then, but it would be improper to do so in public.

Then she took a step back and swiveled to face the house. Sadie gazed at it. Shaun could imagine what memories must be flowing through her mind, and his heart sank even further.

With a look of hope, she asked the dreaded question. "Have you heard from the architect yet? Is there a way to build the hotel without tearing down the house?"

Her look of hope gave way to a look of despair and remorse. She lowered her head and didn't say a word. *She knows.*

Guilt coursed through him, guilt for the terrible thing he had done.

"I'm so sorry...I didn't want to tell you, but the architect visited me this morning. He was very thorough, but assured me there's no way to construct the hotel while leaving the house intact. I'd hoped there would be another way...I really tried."

His words sounded hollow. What else could he do? The entire situation was out of his control, and he'd never felt so traitorous in his life.

With a forced smile Sadie nodded at him. "I'm sure you did. You and your father have a business, and you've planned a hotel, so that's what you must build."

She spun away from him, but Shaun grabbed her arm. "Please let me walk with you." When she didn't reply, he stepped beside her and they walked in silence. At the end of Willow Lane, they turned toward Sadie's cottage. Not a word was spoken as he accompanied her all the way to her home.

When the couple reached the porch of Sadie's cottage, they paused. She didn't invite him inside, but merely thanked him for walking with her.

"I'll be here to see you in the morning. Are you still due at the Riverview dock at nine o'clock?" His heart was hammering, and he again wanted to kiss her. But this was not the time nor place. In her present mood, Sadie most likely wouldn't welcome a kiss from him.

She offered a sad smile. "I'll see you in the morning."

With that, Sadie hurried into her home, leaving Shaun staring at the closed door. Did the closed door signify the end of their relationship?

~ ~ ~ ~

"I know you didn't want a big send-off, Sadie dear. But you're going to be on that ship quite a while, so I had to send some food with you." Dolly Hatcher smiled at Sadie. "Fred is running the store this morning, but he sends his best regards and says he'll be praying for you. The entire town of Riverview will be praying for you. What a fine thing you're doing, sailing across the sea to work with orphans." Dolly dabbed at her eyes with the hem of her apron.

Sadie leaned over and hugged the storekeeper's wife. "Thank you so much. I can't tell you what this means to me." She gestured to the wrapped parcels containing bread, crackers, and her favorite peppermint sticks. "And your prayers, most of all." She didn't have much time before the schooner departed for Savannah, so after saying good-bye again, she hurried inside to add the items to the satchel she'd keep with her on the ship. The treats from Dolly Hatcher would indeed come in handy while sailing.

A few minutes later Shaun arrived, and he, Sadie, and her father climbed into the carriage that Horace had arranged to drive them. The trunk had been loaded on the back, and Sadie sat between her father and Shaun, not saying a word.

She'd already cried when petting her cats again, knowing they would wonder where she was in the coming weeks and months. Now as the carriage jostled them along, her mind repeated her silent prayer. *Oh Lord, please be with Papa while I'm gone. Please help him not be too sad. And please give me the strength I need to face whatever challenges I might have ahead. I'm nervous about being on the sea, and nervous about living in a strange country. But if this is what I'm to do, then I know I must lean on You. And please be with Shaun...I love him so...*

The schooner was waiting at the dock, and after tearful hugs and good-byes, Sadie stood next to her bags, waving to her father and Shaun standing on the dock. Behind them stood Pastor Lucas and his wife, waving and smiling.

Traveling along the river, Sadie sat numbly on one side of the boat, praying. Was she really doing this? Perhaps it was all a dream, and she'd awaken in her own bed in the cottage she shared with her papa. Her beloved cats would be curled up on the foot of her bed, and it would be a normal day in Riverview.

No, it was real, and the schooner was approaching the Savannah port. The busy, bustling seaside seemed like a different world to Sadie. She was accustomed to Riverview, with a slower pace of life. Tears stung her eyes, mixed with the salty air blowing in from the Atlantic Ocean. How could she have any tears remaining? She was following her call to serve in Africa, so her crying should be behind her. Sadie's hair whipped around her shoulders, and she pushed loose strands away from her face.

An older woman on the schooner smiled at Sadie, then reached over and patted her arm. In a gentle voice, the woman asked if she could pray with Sadie. She must have noticed the concern shadowing Sadie's face and her misting eyes.

After the brief prayer, Sadie thanked the woman and drew in a deep breath. *Pray. Trust. Listen.* The words echoed in her mind and she focused on her favorite Bible verse. The wind picked up, blowing wildly around her, as the words replayed in her mind. *I will instruct thee and teach thee in the way which thou shalt go.* And suddenly, clear as a ferry's bell, Sadie knew in her heart what she must do.

~ ~ ~ ~

Shaun rode away from the Riverview dock with Horace Perkins, neither man uttering a word. He felt as though a weight pulled at his heart. Had Sadie really left? To be gone possibly a year—to another country? A country across the ocean. The stark reality made his chest ache.

He shook off selfish thoughts and glanced at Sadie's father, who appeared to be fighting tears. The man had just sent his only daughter off to serve as a missionary with his blessing. What a noble thing to do. Surely his heart was as heavy as Shaun's.

"Mr. Perkins, I'll be checking on you as often as I can, and perhaps we can dine together now and then, my treat. The café in Riverview has some delicious food." Shaun grinned, hoping to lighten the mood.

"Much obliged, son. I'd enjoy having you visit me and joining you at the café once in a while would be a nice change too." Horace's voice was somber.

After the pair arrived at the Perkins' cottage, Shaun bade the older man good-bye, then headed to Miss Callie's. His plan was to return by train to Savannah and meet with his father.

Grabbing his bag from his room, Shaun explained to Miss Callie he'd most likely be away for a few days, so she needn't plan on him being there for meals.

"I know today was the day for Miss Perkins to leave on her missionary journey. It must be hard for you." The woman's two brief statements held much meaning, and her moisture-filled eyes conveyed understanding to Shaun.

He simply nodded, then left for the train station. As he rode the train, he mulled over what he would say to his father. Since the architect hadn't created a plan to keep the house, the next step was having it demolished. He would see if his father wanted to locate another construction company, or if he'd leave it up to Shaun.

At this point, Shaun had lost his enthusiasm for the project. Earning his father's respect and recognition no longer seemed important. The only thing important in his life was his relationship with Sadie, and now she was sailing to Africa. Or would be soon. If the ship hadn't already departed, it likely would still be in the Savannah port, but not much longer.

As the train rolled along, Shaun's mind cleared. He prayed, although prayer was still new to him. A comforting feeling washed over him as he glanced out at the passing scenery. Everything he saw out his train window was God's creation—the fields, trees, and clouds up in the sky. And that same God loved Shaun and wanted him to be happy.

Suddenly, Shaun knew what he had to do. Somehow, he would pay his father for the property on Willow Lane. If Shaun was the owner, then he could allow the house to remain, and share it with Sadie. Her dream house. It would finally be hers, and she could open her home for orphaned children if she still desired.Perhaps if she knew of this change in Shaun's plans, she would have a lighter heart knowing her dream house would still be standing when she returned from Africa. If Shaun could only tell her about his plans in person.

Another thought came to him at that moment, a thought that made his heart pound. Maybe, just maybe the ship hadn't sailed yet, and he could see Sadie and tell her what he planned to do. He leaned forward in his seat, as though doing so would make the train go faster. His entire body tensed, and his pulse raced.

Thankfully, a matter of minutes later the train pulled into the Savannah depot, and Shaun couldn't depart quickly enough. He must get to the port—right away. Hailing a carriage, he grasped his bag and climbed into the vehicle, instructing the driver to please hurry.

Oh Lord, please let the ship still be there. I know You aren't used to me praying, at least not much. But I'm begging you this one request...You know how much I love Sadie and want to spend my life with her. If I can only reach her before the ship sails for Africa and tell her I'm going to buy her dream house for her.

The carriage pulled up to the unloading area near the port. Shaun thanked the driver, giving him a generous tip. Tightly grasping his bag, Shaun raced, panting, toward the dock. He looked at the boats docked there, but saw no big ship. Wait, there was one—maybe that was the one bound for Africa. He must find out right away.

Seeing a dockworker, Shaun stopped him. "Sir, has the ship leaving for Africa sailed yet?" Shaun held his breath as he awaited the reply.

The dockworker stroked his whiskered chin and nodded. "Yep, that ship sailed a little bit ago, sir. Made a big show pulling out of the harbor here. Pretty exciting, thinking of sailing all that way." The man gazed out on the water, devoid of boats.

Shaun's heart may as well have been weighted by an anchor as it plunged to the bottom of his being. The ship was gone...Sadie was gone. And he didn't know when he'd see her again. Now she wouldn't know about his plan to purchase the house and land on Willow Lane. Her time in Africa would be spent thinking that when she returned home, her beloved house would be gone. Maybe she wouldn't come back, now that there was nothing to come home to, now that her dream was demolished by his doing.

With his steps dragging on the pavement, Shaun turned

to hail another carriage that would take him to his father's office. His mind—and his heart—were not ready to think about business matters today. All he could think of was the beautiful woman he loved, now on a ship sailing to another continent.

Worries that he had previously ignored and shoved down deep now began to surface. What if Sadie met someone in Africa and fell in love? There would be other missionaries working alongside her, and many of them would certainly be men.

Shaun felt like he'd been punched in the gut and hoped he wouldn't become physically ill while in the carriage. The road was rough, and the driver had to swerve several times to avoid holes. Overhead, the sky was gray and dreary, matching Shaun's mood.

When he arrived at his father's building, Shaun paid the driver, clutched his bag and went inside the office. Several workers greeted him, but Shaun's replies were lackluster. He hoped none of them took offense, but he was miserable at the moment.

"What on earth—are you ill?" The words spewed out of George O'Leary's mouth when he saw his son. His father was looking at him with a mixture of concern and confusion.

Shaun shook his head, placed his bag on the floor, and dropped into a nearby chair. "No Father, I'm not ill. Just not feeling well." When his father didn't comment but continued staring at him, Shaun emitted a loud sigh.

"Remember the woman I told you about? Sadie?"

George O'Leary nodded, and a hint of a smile crossed his face. "Yes, the woman who has special ties to the house on our property. The same house that's to be demolished."

"Yes. She left on a ship for Africa this morning and will most likely be gone for a year. Maybe longer." Shaun cleared his throat, not wanting to appear like a lovesick schoolboy but hoping his father would understand, at least a little.

"Anyway, the architect wasn't able to draw an alternate plan for the hotel, so the house will still need to be torn down." Shaun drew in a deep breath and looked his father directly in the eye. "I want to purchase that land from you, Father. I want that land, and that house. Even though I don't presently have the funds, I can give you payments over time—with interest. I will help you locate another suitable piece of land for the hotel." There. He'd said it, and more importantly, Shaun meant what he'd said. They were not empty words or promises. Shaun was compelled to own the land so he could give the house to Sadie.

Silence hung in the air, and George frowned, rubbed his chin, and paced a few steps. Then he slowly turned to face his son.

"You're serious, aren't you?"

"Yes sir, more serious than I've been about anything in my life."

More silence. The clock ticked loud in the office. Funny that Shaun had never noticed it before now. He remained seated, afraid if he stood his legs might give out.

"Well, I must say...I'm proud of you, son. You've decided what you want, and you're pursuing it."

Shaun's eyes widened and his mouth dropped open. This was not the reaction he'd expected from his father.

"You're proud of me?" In disbelief, he repeated the words as a question, certain he must've misunderstood his father. Shaun had been prepared for a battle, not praise. And not from the man who had never acted pleased with anything Shaun had done—or tried to do.

"Yes, that's right. I can tell you care about this woman. And you want to please her. Since the house is so special to her, you're willing to do whatever possible to make her happy, even if she is sailing across the ocean."

Shaun couldn't speak, couldn't respond. The momentous words of his father—the ones he'd been waiting to hear his entire life—left him speechless. Anything he said would sound trite.

"Since the financial success of my company doesn't hinge on this single hotel project, I should be able to agree to your offer. You can pay me for the land over time, but no interest. As your father, I insist on that. I may be a stern businessman, but I'm not a tyrant." George's mouth quirked up at the corners. Then he cleared his throat. "We can begin searching for another property for the hotel. Actually, I already have some good leads. In Darien and closer to Brunswick there might be available land we could purchase, according to some of my sources."

An immense relief swept over Shaun. Although he was still devastated that Sadie was gone, he could work on surprising her with her dream house when she returned.

For the next half hour Shaun and his father discussed drawing up the papers to make the transfer in ownership legal, and even shook hands to seal the deal. Shaun explained he would still need to return to Riverview to check on Horace Perkins. "I promised Sadie I would do that, and I must keep my word. Besides, Mr. Perkins is a nice man, and I enjoy visiting with him."

Shaun caught the next train to Riverview that day. He had a feeling Miss Callie wouldn't mind him showing up again. The woman always treated him kindly and enjoyed the compliments he lavished on her cooking.

Shaun dozed on the train ride, something he normally didn't do. But after the day he'd had, emotionally drained and already missing Sadie so much, he was exhausted.

When the porter called out, Shaun jolted awake. His stomach rumbled, reminding him he'd hardly eaten that day. Hopefully, he would arrive at Miss Callie's in time for the evening meal.

But what would Riverview be like without Sadie? His heart was heavy with pain. How would he get by without seeing her for so long? He trudged along the sidewalk to the boardinghouse, each step taking effort. *Is this what each day would be like while Sadie was gone?*

~ ~ ~ ~

Had she done the right thing? Yes, she was certain. The kind woman who sat beside her on the schooner to Savannah told her she must follow her heart. The woman even prayed with Sadie, and in a moment, it came to her. She could serve the Lord in Riverview. But would everyone be shocked? Or worse yet, disappointed?

Surely no one would judge her. She'd pay back the money that had been raised for her ship voyage, since the ticket had not been used. Once she was reimbursed, she'd take the funds to Pastor Lucas and he could in turn give the money to the church members who'd donated.

Most importantly, after praying and making her decision, Sadie had peace. A complete peace she'd not had previously when she thought of serving as a missionary overseas.

After arriving in Savannah, Mrs. Allen, the woman who'd prayed with Sadie, remained with her as she worked out arrangements to return to Riverview. She assured Sadie that she'd only taken the schooner to Savannah to visit relatives, so she didn't need to rush.

"You've been more than kind to me, Mrs. Allen. I'm certain the Lord used you to help me see clearly what I need to do."

The woman smiled, then softly replied with words Sadie would always remember. "The Lord uses all of us. It might not be in a dramatic or major way—such as being a missionary or being the leader of many people. The Lord places us where we need to be, and He uses us there." She'd patted Sadie's arm, then continued to stay by her side as she worked through details of canceling her passage on the ship and securing a train ticket to Riverview.

As Sadie's trunk was loaded onto the train and she

prepared to climb aboard, she turned to Mrs. Allen. "Thank you so very much. I'll never forget how you helped me."

The older woman hugged her gently, then pulled back. "Just pray for me. And I'll do the same for you." A smile made her eyes sparkle, and she stepped away from the platform.

Sadie climbed onto the train, located her seat next to a window, and almost collapsed. She was drained—physically and emotionally. But all was well, because Sadie Elizabeth Perkins knew exactly what she was supposed to do. She headed home.

~ ~ ~ ~

The next morning Shaun awakened to sun streaming in his bedroom window at the boardinghouse. The aroma of frying bacon and eggs lured him from the bed, and a quick glance at his watch showed he needed to be up and ready for the day.

To accomplish what? The silent voice in his mind taunted him, and the events of the previous day tumbled back through his mind, almost making him want to pull the covers over his head and remain there.

His father was proud of him. Who would have thought? And George O'Leary was selling the property to his son and another location would be purchased for the hotel construction. Finally, after years of feeling he could never please his father, he'd actually said he was proud. Words that Shaun didn't ever think he would hear.

Before leaving Savannah the previous day, Shaun was given the task of viewing several possible locations, and the list of viewings was in his pocket. Two were in the Darien area, so after breakfast he planned to rent a carriage and drive over to take a look.

As he ate the delicious breakfast at Miss Callie's table, the woman eyed him with concern. Was she worried about him? That wouldn't surprise him, since Sadie had left Riverview. He had to admit to himself he appreciated Miss Callie's concern, and he'd become attached to the motherly figure. Perhaps in a way she was similar to Maude, whom he missed while away from Savannah.

"Miss Callie, the breakfast was tasty, as usual." Shaun winked at her. A light blush colored her cheeks. She grabbed the dirty dishes from the table, her head lowered. Although the other boarders complimented her cooking now and then, no one praised her as much as Shaun. Apparently the woman reveled in the attention.

She stopped by his chair. "I'm happy you enjoyed it. Do you have a busy day planned?"

Shaun nodded, reaching out to steady a saucer she was holding along with several other plates. "My plans are to rent a carriage and drive over to Darien. I need to take a look at some land over there, at my father's request. But I should be here for the evening meal."

"That will be just fine. I have a great dinner planned." With that, she retreated into the kitchen.

Shaun stood and headed toward the door. Upon reaching it, he had a change of heart. The last thing he wanted to do today was look at property. Perhaps later in the day or the next day. Right now he only wanted to walk outside and breathe in the fresh air. And take in the sights in Riverview. Shaun had to admit he'd really grown fond of the small town, and not only because Sadie lived there.

She used to live in Riverview—not anymore. The sobering reminder that the woman he loved was on a ship bound for Africa was almost too much to bear. His steps trudged along, his previous lighter mood now evaporated. Thinking of Sadie on a ship in the Atlantic Ocean made Shaun feel almost sick. Why did she have to go? Couldn't she serve the Lord closer to home?

Guilt washed over him. He shouldn't be thinking of himself. Sadie had a heart for God, and was going to help precious children in another country. All because of her love for Jesus, and her calling to be a missionary. He should be proud of her, and he was. It was because he loved her so much that he wanted her to remain in Riverview with him.

He slowed his steps at the corner of Willow Lane. Now that he was purchasing the land from his father, he could view it differently. The land and house were his now, and there would not be a hotel constructed on that site. But what good was that house without Sadie? That was her dream house, but now she was far away.

With his heart heavier than ever, Shaun inched along the sidewalk, each step bringing him closer to the land that was now his. The lovely house that wouldn't be demolished after all, which he was thankful for. After all, it truly was a beautiful, stately house and would make a wonderful home for someone. Sadie—that would be her house.

Perhaps he could begin making plans to work on the house, so when Sadie returned home months from now, it would be ready for her to occupy. That would help him connect to the beautiful woman, despite the fact she was a continent away from him.

He reached the property, and stood for a few moments on the sidewalk, studying the house. Sunlight streamed between the trees, and birds chirped a chorus as if welcoming him to his new home. It was a lovely structure indeed, and after renovations were made, it would be spectacular.

Movement from the left side of the house caught his eye. Someone else was here. As long as the person didn't bother anything, Shaun didn't mind someone walking around on his land. After all, it was a peaceful setting.

The person was a woman. Her steps were dainty and tentative over the rough ground as she circled the front of house. She lifted her skirt, and her long hair hung loosely around her slender shoulders. The woman glanced up, and her eyes locked with his.

Sadie! The woman walking around the property must be a figment of his broken heart. No, it wasn't possible. His eyes and mind must be playing tricks on him. The recent events had taken a toll, and now he was imagining things. It couldn't be Sadie, because she was on a ship bound for Africa. At that very moment she'd be in the middle of the Atlantic Ocean, and Shaun only hoped the seas weren't choppy and rough.

He continued staring. His breath caught and he blinked his eyes. Now she was walking toward him. It was Sadie—it was really her!

Hardly believing his eyes, Shaun sprinted toward her, then grabbed her in his arms.

"Sadie, Sadie. My beautiful Sadie." No other words would come from his mouth at the moment. He only wanted to utter her name and clutch her close to him. He didn't ever want to let her go.

With a giggle, Sadie gasped. "Shaun, I can't breathe—" She gasped again.

"Oh," he released his tight grip but didn't completely let go of her. He couldn't. Having the woman he loved now standing inches from him was more than he could've asked for, and he wasn't about to let her go.

The couple gazed into each other's eyes, not speaking for a few seconds. Then Shaun leaned down and kissed her, a powerful, yet tender kiss.

"Sadie, what are you doing here? I thought you were sailing to Africa." Before she could respond he planted another kiss, then kissed the tip of her nose, making her giggle again. "But whatever happened, I'm so thankful you're here. And I can't let you go, Sadie. Please say you'll stay here in Riverview, and we'll be married."

Breathless, Sadie looked up at him in wide-eyed wonder. "Yes, I'm staying in Riverview. And I would love to marry you. Don't worry, I'll tell you everything that happened to me since we said good-bye yesterday. That will explain why

I'm back in Riverview. I hadn't planned on walking to this house, but it just seemed to beckon me…it's hard to explain, but as I've shared with you before, this house has special meaning to me." Her green eyes held a faraway look.

Shaun drew his head back and beamed at her. "I'm glad this house is special to you, because soon it will become even more special to you."

When she appeared puzzled at his words, Shaun continued.

"Sadie, I am buying this land—and this house—to be your house. *Our house*, after we're married. There will not be a hotel built on this land. We'll fix up this house exactly as you want it, and Lord willing, one day we'll fill it with children. Whether they're orphans we adopt, or children you give birth to, they'll be our children." He smiled at her, his heart about to burst with the love he felt for this precious woman.

"You've made me the happiest person in the world. My dream is coming true—except it's coming true even better than I could've imagined. I'll be proud to be your wife, and live in this lovely house filled with children. With the Lord at the center of our marriage, we'll build a life together that will be a dream-come-true."

EPILOGUE

Sadie and Shaun couldn't have asked for a more beautiful wedding day—or wedding ceremony. As Sadie spoke her vows and gazed into the eyes of her groom on that August day, she was the happiest woman on earth.

Lucy and Matthew, who'd married the previous month, beamed from the front row with Sadie's papa.

Although Sadie had been concerned about meeting Shaun's parents, things went well. As predicted, his sister Maggie and the housekeeper Maude adored her right away. The feeling was mutual. George and Colleen O'Leary embraced Sadie and referred to her as their new daughter. Shaun winked at Sadie when his parents spoke that term of endearment.

After the ceremony, the couple rode away in a horse-drawn carriage to spend their first night as man and wife in a secluded cabin on the outskirts of Riverview.

"Your father was so kind to arrange for a cabin for us." Sadie looked lovingly at the handsome man seated next to her in the carriage.

"He was happy to do so—and besides, it belongs to a

business acquaintance of his. My father has helped the man in the past, so it all works out." He kissed her forehead. "Speaking of things working out, I'm also glad that your papa is willing to let us live with him while we renovate our house on Willow Lane. I liked your father from the first moment I met him."

Hearing her groom speak so kindly of her beloved father, Sadie felt a warmth down to her toes that had nothing to do with the temperature of the summertime coastal air.

"Papa is fond of you too. And he'll be happy to have us living with him a while, and even once we move into our own house, we won't be far away from Papa, so I can check on him often."

Shaun's eyes held a mischievous gleam. "Hmm...that will work out well, especially after we start filling up our home with children. I have a feeling your papa will make a wonderful grandpa."

Sadie didn't think her smile could be any wider, or her heart full of any more love. She snuggled closer to Shaun as the coastal breeze began to blow, so thankful the Lord had blessed her with this amazing husband.

Now more than ever, she'd learned the Lord gives His children what they need, and even when dreams don't go as planned, they can still come true.

THE END

Patti Jo Moore is a former kindergarten teacher who now writes full-time. Her "Sweet, Southern Stories" feature characters who face realistic struggles and challenging situations but always have a happily-ever-after ending.

Patti Jo loves Jesus, her family, cats, and coffee. When not writing, she loves spending time with her family—especially her precious grandbaby. She enjoys connecting with readers and can be found on Facebook at Author Patti Jo Moore. You can also visit her blog at http://catmomscorner.blogspot.com

She has three contemporary stories and one historical, all with Forget-Me-Not Romances.

Made in the USA
Monee, IL
14 September 2019